I

Jinx, the cat, was asleep on an old sofa cushion behind the stove in the kitchen. Jinx was very fond of the sofa cushion. Mrs. Bean, the farmer's wife, had made it for him out of a red satin dress she had had when she was a girl, and she had embroidered his name on it in blue worsted and there was a border of blue forget-me-nots around the edge. Robert, the collie, and Georgie, the little brown dog, slept on the other side of the stove, but had only pieces of carpet. And the four mice—Eek and Quik and Eeny and Cousin Augustus—who sometimes came into the kitchen to sleep in cold weather, had just an old cigar box of Mr. Bean's with some rags in it.

It was a raw blustery March night and the wind kept going round and round the house, trying the doors and rattling the windows to make sure that everything was locked up tight. It would rush away across the fields and everything would be quiet for a while, then pretty soon it would come rushing back as if it had forgotten something, and would rattle the doors and windows all over again.

After a while it found a loose shutter on the front parlor window and began banging it. It banged it and shook it and rattled it and tried to pull it off the hinges. And that seemed to excite the wind. It began to play with the house as a cat does with a ball. It would go 'way off and be very quiet for a while, creeping up slowly on the house, and then suddenly it would leap on it and shake it. Or it would go high up in the star-lit sky and drop on the house with a bang. It roared down the chimney and blew under the doors so that the carpets rippled along the floor, and it slapped the windows and whistled through the keyholes. And at last Jinx woke up and said: "My goodness, can't we have a little peace and quiet around here?"

"Oh, I don't know," said Robert. "I kind of like to

lie here all snug and warm and listen to the wind."

"There's always too much noise around here," said Jinx. "If it isn't one thing it's another. There, just listen to that."

There had come a lull in the wind and in it they could hear a faint little regular moan. It was Cousin Augustus snoring.

"Well, surely you don't mind that tonight, Jinx, with all this racket going on," said Georgie.

"Those darn mice!" said Jinx. "They can sleep through anything." He got up and stretched, and then reached out a paw and shut the cover of the cigar box with a smack.

At once there was a great squeaking and rustling in the box and then the mice came tumbling out. "Hey, Jinx! Robert!" they squeaked. "Who did that? Help! What's the matter?"

Jinx just sat and laughed at them, but Robert said: "Go on back to bed, boys. That was just Jinx's idea of a joke." And then he stopped and listened for a second and said: "Psst! Here comes Mr. Bean."

The wind was rattlety-bang-banging away against the shutter and they couldn't hear Mr. Bean, but the back stairs began to get light as if somebody was coming with a candle. First they saw a large blue and yellow carpet slipper on the top step. And then another slipper jumped past it onto the step below. The slippers kept coming down like this and pretty soon they saw a long white nightshirt, and then a face which was mostly all whiskers with a nose sticking out of them and two sharp eyes looking over them, and then a white nightcap with a red tassel. And last of all they saw an arm that ended in a hand holding a lighted candle. And Mr. Bean was in the kitchen.

He went through the kitchen into the front parlor and they heard him put up the window and fasten the loose blind. Then he came back. The dogs thumped their tails on the floor, and Jinx got up and rubbed his left ear on Mr. Bean's leg. Mr. Bean looked at them.

"I suppose you animals would let that blind bang itself to pieces before you'd get up and fasten it," he said. "I go round tellin' all and sundry that my animals are the smartest animals in New York State, but I dunno. Seems to me if you was so all-fired smart you'd fix a little thing like that yourselves without waiting for me to do it. My gracious, if I can't count on you to see to a little thing like that, how could I go off to Europe all summer like Mrs. Bean wants me to, and leave you in charge of the farm? No, no; 'tain't to be thought of." And he stumped off upstairs again.

• • • then the mice came tumbling out • • •

"Oh, dear," said Georgie, "I knew something like this would happen. Mrs. Bean has worked so hard to get him to promise to take her and the boys to Europe."

"I wish we *had* thought to fasten the old blind," said Jinx. "But, after all, it's a pretty small thing to put off the trip to Europe for."

"Well, I don't know," said Robert. "I don't believe any other farmer would ever go away and leave his farm in charge of a lot of animals for six months. It isn't that we can't look after things and keep the farm going all right. But animals aren't used to taking any responsibility. When we see something that ought to be done we usually wait for Mr. Bean to do something about it. Just like that blind."

"Well," said Jinx, "we *can* look after the farm all right. But will we? You know how it is when we're all responsible for seeing to something. Each one of us thinks: 'Oh, well, somebody else will look after that.' And then it never gets done. No, we've got to select one animal who will be responsible for everything."

"But there isn't any one animal who could do all the work on the farm," said Georgie.

"I don't mean he'd *do* all the work. But he'd see

that it got done—tell all the others what to do. Well, like the President of the United States. He'd be the big boss."

"He'd be President of the Bean Farm," said Georgie. "Say, Jinx, why couldn't we elect a president? Have a regular election and everything?"

"Golly, that's a good idea!" said Jinx enthusiastically. "An election with torchlight processions and campaign speeches and everything! That would fix running the farm, all right. And we'd have a lot of fun too. We'll get hold of Freddy first thing in the morning and call a meeting and talk it over."

"There are a lot of things about running a farm that we don't know, though," said Robert. "There's money. What do any of us know about money?"

"I found a quarter once," said Georgie.

"What did you do with it?" asked Robert.

"I don't remember."

"There you are," said Jinx. "He doesn't remember. And yet you know what Mr. Bean said yesterday to Mrs. Bean about Adoniram? 'That boy,' he said, 'has got to learn to take care of money, or he'll never make a farmer.' Well, we won't be good farmers either if we don't learn."

"How do you take care of money?" Quik asked.

"Put it in the bank, silly," said Jinx.

"What for?" said Quik.

"Oh, how should I know?" said the cat crossly. "Anyway, what do you care, mouse? You haven't got any money."

"Is that so?" said Quik. "You'd be surprised how many pieces of money mice find back of baseboards and under floors and places."

"I suppose that's so," said Robert. "I wish there was some way we could show Mr. Bean we knew how to take care of money. That would make him feel better than anything about going away and leaving us to look after the farm."

"Perhaps we could start a bank," said Georgie.

"That's an idea," said the cat. "Gosh, you're full of ideas tonight, Georgie. If we were bankers, Mr. Bean wouldn't worry, I bet. I've often heard him say that the bankers were the backbone of the country."

"Yes, but how do you start a bank?" asked Eeny.

"Pooh! Nothing to it!" said the cat. "You just— well, you just open it. Big sign over the door— 'BANK.' That's all."

"Oh," said Eeny. "So you call it a bank and then it's a bank, hey?"

"Sure."

"Oh," said Eeny again. "So then if I call you a big blowhard, what does that make you?"

"What!" yelled Jinx. "Why, you—" He made a dive for the cigar box, but the mice had sneaked away in the darkness, and in a pause in the wind he heard them giggling together under the floor. For a minute he didn't say anything. He couldn't see the two dogs. Cats can see better than other animals in the dark but they can't see when there isn't any light at all, and the kitchen was as dark as a bottom bureau drawer. He listened suspiciously, but the wind made so much noise again that he couldn't tell whether the dogs were laughing or not. After a minute he said: "Darned mice! I don't know why I put up with them."

"Well," said Robert, "if you will try to pretend that you know about things when you don't, you must expect to be made fun of. The bank's a good idea, though. We might find out from Mr. Webb how to run it."

"Old Webb?" said Jinx. "What would a spider know about banking!"

"He used to live in a bank before he came out to the farm," said Robert. "Golly, listen to that wind!"

Indeed, the wind, after a short rest, was now more violent than ever. It wasn't playing any more. It seemed to have lost its temper completely, and it whacked and boomed like big guns, so that the whole house shook. Around and around the house it went, whooping and banging, and all at once there came a louder crash and the latch of the kitchen door gave way and the door flew open, letting in a gust of cold wind that swept through the kitchen, setting the window curtains flying and the pots and pans clattering.

The animals made a rush to push the door shut again. They threw their weight against it and shoved. Even the mice dug in their toes and heaved, for every little helps, even if it's only a four-mouse-power push. And when the wind slackened a little, they got the door shut. The dogs dragged up a chair and pushed and hauled until they had the back wedged under the doorknob. And then they all said: "Whee!" and lay down again.

And then a light began to glow in the backstairs doorway and Mr. Bean appeared again. He appeared in the same order as before—slippers, nightshirt, whiskers, nightcap, arm and candle. And he looked around for a minute and then said: "H'm. You showed some sense this time." And he gave Robert a friendly whack on the side and then disappeared again—candle, nightcap, whiskers, nightshirt, and last of all the slippers.

Well, that was high praise from Mr. Bean. He was fond of his animals, but he never paid them compliments.

"That makes up for forgetting the blind," said Robert. "I hope he'll think we're more responsible now. But what do you say we try to get a little sleep?"

It was quieter again now. They could hear the wind rushing farther and farther away into the distance, as if it had finally decided to abandon the attack against a house that was so well guarded and to hunt for another victim. The animals curled up in their beds and drew in their breaths to give a long comfortable sigh. And just at that minute from the far corner of the room there came a weak squawk.

Now, a squawk, no matter how faint, in a dark room in the middle of the night is pretty scary. If Jinx had been alone he would have walked right out of that kitchen—at least he would have started to walk, but he would probably have been running by the time he reached the door—and he would have gone down cellar and hid behind the cider barrel. But the other animals were there, and he had a reputation to keep up as a bold, free, fearless sort of fellow. So he said very sternly: "Come, come, what's this?" and went straight over to investigate. Most brave people are like Jinx. They're brave because they're afraid to act scared.

Jinx went over to the refrigerator and put his nose down under it and sniffed three little cat-sniffs. And behind him Robert and Georgie sniffed too—loud dog-sniffs. "Feathers!" said Jinx. "A bird," said Robert.

"Wind must have blown him in the door," said Georgie.

"Help!" said something under the refrigerator in a weak little squawk.

So Jinx reached under and caught a leg and pulled, and as soon as the bird was out he tried to stand up. But he was so exhausted that he fell over on his side.

"Take it easy, brother," said Jinx. "Over to the stove, boys, and get him warm. Careful, there. You take his legs, Georgie. That's the stuff."

"Let me handle him," said Robert, and he picked the bird up gently in his mouth and carried him over and put him in the warm cigar box.

"Oh, that wind!" murmured the bird.

"What's your name, bird?" Jinx asked. "You a stranger in these parts?"

"Let him alone," said Robert. "Let him rest. You can ask him questions in the morning."

"O.K.," said Jinx, and lay down again on his cushion. "Well, *now* maybe I can get some sleep."

The wind didn't come back again, and in a little while the only sounds in the kitchen were the faint moaning of the stranger in his sleep and the gentle snoring of Cousin Augustus, who, deprived of the cigar-box bed, had curled up to sleep with his three cousins between Robert's forepaws.

II

The animals had had a hard night, and when Mrs. Bean came down in the morning to get breakfast for Mr. Bean and the two boys they had adopted, Byram and Adoniram, they were still sound asleep.

Mrs. Bean was a short, plump little woman, with snapping black eyes and cheeks that really were like apples. You no more knew what she looked like without an apron than you knew what Mr. Bean looked like without his whiskers. The animals all loved her and she was very fond of them and was always fixing little extra surprises for their supper. And she even baked them a cake on their birthdays. Except for Mrs.

Wogus, who didn't like cake, she baked a birthday apple pie. Mrs. Wogus was one of the cows.

As soon as Jinx woke up he yawned, and then without stopping to wash his face he crawled under the stove and looked in the cigar box. "Well, my goodness," he said, "I guess you're all right." For the bird was sitting up and preening his feathers. He was a handsome woodpecker with a red head and a black and white body.

"Thanks to you," said the bird politely. "And would you mind telling me where I am?"

"Why, you're in a cigar box under the stove in Mrs. Bean's kitchen," said Jinx.

"No, no, you misunderstand me," said the woodpecker. "I want to know what part of the country I am in. You see, I was coming north to spend the summer in our old family home in Washington when I was caught in that windstorm, and I am afraid it has blown me a long way off my course."

"I'll say it has," said the cat. "Why, you're up in the middle of New York State."

"New York State?" said the woodpecker. "Dear me, I was never very good at geography. Just where is New York State?"

"Hey, look," said Jinx. "Are you trying to tell me

you don't know where New York State is?"

"I'm not trying to tell you, I *am* telling you," said the woodpecker. "It's not quite the same thing."

"Maybe it isn't," said the cat, who was beginning to get confused. "But I must say—"

But just then Mrs. Bean bent down and looked under the stove.

"What's going on under here?" she said. "Oh, it's you, Jinx. And—my land, a woodpecker! Well, you'd better go on outside. It's all right for you to entertain your friends in the house, but my kitchen's no place for a woodpecker. You know how Mr. Bean feels about birds in the house. He don't like 'em flying about. He's afraid they'll get in his whiskers. I dare say it's unreasonable of him, but there it is. Come, outside, both of you."

She held open the door and Jinx and the woodpecker went out, followed by the two dogs, who had waked up and had been listening with interest to the conversation.

"Do you really mean you don't know where New York State is?" asked Robert, when they were in the barnyard and the woodpecker had flown up onto the trunk of a big elm and begun drilling a hole in the bark to see if he could get a little breakfast.

18

"Certainly I mean it," he said. He gave a few taps with his bill, knocking off a bit of bark, then pulled out a small bug and ate it. "H'm," he said, "very tender. Very tasty. In Washington, you see," he went on, "we really can't keep track of all the little unimportant places out on the edge of such a big country."

"Oh, is that so!" said Jinx. "Seems to me you talk pretty big for a woodpecker. I suppose you're somebody pretty important down in Washington. I suppose we ought to know who you are."

"You may have seen my picture in the newspapers," said the woodpecker. "It has been in several times. We are rather a famous family. We have had our home in a sycamore on the White House lawn for many generations. And the eldest son is always named after one of the presidents. The founder of our family was named Abraham. My grandfather, Woodrow, was quite famous. As an egg, he fell out of the nest. The President himself was passing beneath at the time and Woodrow fell into his pocket. He was carried into the White House and hatched out in the pocket the next day, where he was found by a servant and taken outdoors again. So that Woodrow was actually born in the White House. My own name," he added, "is John Quincy."

The dogs were rather awed at having such a distinguished visitor in the barnyard, and even Jinx was impressed. But he wasn't going to show it. He shrugged his shoulders and gave a sort of nasty laugh and strolled off in the direction of the cow-barn, leaving the dogs to continue the conversation.

The three cows, Mrs. Wiggins, Mrs. Wogus, and Mrs. Wurzburger, were out having their breakfast in the back pasture. But Jinx went into the barn. In a far corner a strand of spider web was hanging down, and the cat pulled at it gently with one paw, for it was Mr. Webb's doorbell. In a minute a small spider came hurrying down the strand and stopped just opposite Jinx's ear. This was Mrs. Webb. She was a plump round little spider who rather prided herself on her resemblance to Mrs. Bean, and indeed there was a certain likeness in their plumpness and the way they bustled about, although they did not look much like each other in the face.

"Good morning, Jinx," said the spider. "Webb's off for his morning walk. Anything I can do?" She had a brisk, pleasant voice, though it was very small. Spiders are very talkative, but few people know it, for they have to get almost in your ear to make themselves heard, and they don't like to do it much because they know it tickles.

"Just a matter of business," said the cat. "Which way did he go?"

"The roof, I guess. Go right up."

Mr. Webb, who was rather stout, liked to take regular exercise to keep his figure down. But in the early spring it was too wet underfoot to do much walking, so he usually took his walks on the roof of the cow-barn. Four times around the edge of the roof was a spider's mile. Jinx found him sitting on the peak of the roof with four of his legs dangling over the barn-yard.

There was nothing Mr. Webb liked to do better than talk about his banking experiences, and so for an hour or more he went on and on and Jinx listened attentively. But of course what the cat wanted to know was how to start a bank, and hearing all about the time the robber came into the bank and Mr. Webb bit him on the leg and made him run away, or about the terrible fight Mr. Webb had with the black caterpillars who started to eat up the paper money, wasn't much good to him. So finally he said: "Yes, yes, that's all very interesting, but how do you start a bank?"

"Start a bank?" said Mr. Webb. "Nothing easier. You just start it, that's all. Then people bring you their money and you keep it safe for them. Then when they want to get some out, they write a check."

"What's that?" Jinx asked.

"Well," said Mr. Webb, "suppose I have some money in your bank and I want to pay Robert forty cents I owe him. I don't go and get the money and give it to him. I give him a check that says: 'Jinx's Bank. Pay to Robert, forty cents.' And I sign it with my name. And he brings it to you and you give him the money."

"I don't believe any of the animals I know would let me keep their money for them," said Jinx thoughtfully. "Even if they had any."

"Well, frankly," said Mr. Webb, "I don't think they would either. Nobody doubts your honesty, Jinx. I don't mean that. But you're up to too many tricks. No, you'd have to have somebody else as president of the bank, somebody they'd feel was thoroughly reliable, like Mrs. Wiggins. Or somebody with a big name. Did I ever tell you about the time President Harding—"

"Yes, you did," Jinx interrupted. "But that reminds me. Who do you suppose blew in last night? John Quincy Adams."

"John Quincy—what?" exclaimed Mr. Webb. "Oh,

come, Jinx, you don't mean to tell me—"

"I do, though," said Jinx. "That's his name. Only he's just a woodpecker." And he told the spider about it.

Mr. Webb was much excited. "But good gracious, Jinx, he's just the one to be president of your bank. Don't you see? 'Jinx's Bank. President: John Quincy Adams.' Why, every animal for miles around will want to have an account in that bank. Can't you get him to stay and be president?"

"Gosh, that's an idea," said the cat. "Thanks, Webb. See you later." And Jinx hurried off back to the barn-yard, where quite a number of the animals had gathered to admire the distinguished visitor.

The distinguished visitor, however, had now climbed so far up among the leaves of the elm that he was invisible from the ground. They could hear the tap, tap of his strong beak, and an occasional "De-licious!" as he ate another bug.

"Hi, John Quincy!" shouted Jinx. "Come down here a minute. I've got a proposition to make to you."

The woodpecker flew down and perched on a low limb. "Really, my friends," he said, "I must apolo-gize to you for knowing so little about your won-derful state. Your bugs are really marvelous." He

23

smacked his beak. "Such crispness! Such flavor—full, yet delicate! I am half tempted to stay here for a time if you will permit me, to feast on these delicacies."

"I'm glad to hear you say that," said Jinx. And then he told him about the bank, and that he wanted him to be president.

"It is a great honor," said the woodpecker. "But I will be frank with you. I know very little about banking."

"We don't know anything about it, either," said Jinx, "so I don't see that that makes much difference."

"Well," said John Quincy, "you tempt me. I admit you tempt me. Washington can be very tiring. The balls, the parties, the political conferences, the diplomatic intrigues—one grows weary of the constant round of gaiety. I have often thought that I should like to spend a summer among the plain country people, sharing their simple pleasures. And perhaps—who knows?—my wide experience and deep knowledge of men and cities might be of some help to them too. Yes, I accept."

"Good," said Jinx. "Then come along and talk to Freddy with me. I have to see him anyway this morning about our election."

"Who's Freddy, if I may ask?" said the woodpecker.

"Freddy? Oh, he's just—Freddy. He's a detective and a poet and—oh, lots of things. He'll have to be our secretary, because he's the only animal on the farm that can read or write. He's a pig."

"A pig!" exclaimed John Quincy, and he laughed heartily. "Dear me, I *am* going to be rural and no mistake. A pig! Well, well!"

III

The next two weeks were very busy ones on the Bean farm. The idea of electing a president was enthusiastically received. It would be a great thing, the animals all felt, to found the first animal republic. Of course none of them knew very much about how to start a republic, or how to hold an election, but Freddy read up about it in his encyclopedia, and John Quincy was a great help too. For of course, living in Washington, the woodpecker knew all about government.

Freddy and Jinx and some of the others were all

for holding the election right away, but when John Quincy heard of this he said he thought they ought to wait until they had got the bank started.

"Oh, you just say that because you are to be president of the bank," said Freddy.

"Dear me," said John Quincy, "I am in no hurry for that, I assure you. No, it merely occurs to me that your main reason for starting a republic is so that the farm will be well run in Mr. Bean's absence. But Mr. Bean isn't planning to go abroad for another month, so I am told, and in the meantime, if you don't convince him that you are capable of taking on such a responsible job, he may not go at all. The quickest way to convince him is to start your bank."

"Well, why can't we do both right away?" asked Jinx.

"Because it will take longer to get the bank going," said the woodpecker. "Anybody can start a republic in five minutes. But a bank—well, you haven't even got any safe-deposit vaults yet."

"Safe-deposit vaults?" said Freddy.

"Sure," said John Quincy. "That's what a bank has to have. Burglar-proof vaults. Underground, with steel doors and somebody to guard them. For money and valuables."

27

They were going to have the bank in an old tool-shed that stood by the side of the road some distance from the house. So Jinx hired a family of woodchucks that lived in the upper pasture to come down and dig some vaults under the shed. They dug a tunnel about twenty-five feet long, big enough for Jinx to crawl through, and at the end they dug two rooms: a smaller room for money and a larger room for valuables. They put a board over the opening to the tunnel, and who-ever was on guard sat on it.

The day the bank opened for business Freddy brought out the sign he had painted and they hung it up. It read:

FIRST ANIMAL BANK OF CENTERBORO

President: John Quincy Adams *Treasurer:* Jinx
Secretary: Freddy

Capital: None yet *Resources:* Unlimited

These names are the guarantee of your secu-rity. Why worry about the safety of your money and valuables? Bring them to us and let us do the worrying. Do business with the old reliable firm.

For the first few days the bank was crowded from

dawn to dusk. Animals came from miles around to open accounts, or to leave valuables in safekeeping. Most of them came out of curiosity, to see how a bank worked, or to have a talk with its distinguished president, but of course they all brought something. There was a line at the door that extended away off down the road. And as each one came in, John Quincy would talk with him for a minute, explaining how the bank worked, and then Freddy would write down in a notebook what they had brought, and one of the squirrels whom they had engaged as cashiers and clerks would take it down to the vaults. By the end of the third day there was $21.03 in the money room, and the valuables room was so full that there wasn't space for anything more.

"It's a good thing the entrance to the vaults is so small," said Jinx. "Suppose we'd had to take in things like that ox-yoke that that cow from Lakeville wanted us to keep for her because her great-uncle used to wear it!"

"We have to draw the line at foodstuffs, too," said John Quincy. "I turned away several dogs that came in with bones. And squirrels have been bringing in thousands of nuts. What kind of a bank is that to be president of—one that has its vaults full of nuts?"

"Well, for that matter," said Freddy, "what kind of a bank is it that doesn't charge for its services? I vote we charge a cent a month on all accounts."

As soon as this monthly charge was announced, business fell off badly. But although most animals haven't much use for money, they can always get a little if they need it. In a district that has been settled for a hundred and fifty years, many thousands of coins have been lost. They have slipped from purses, dropped through holes in pockets, fallen through cracks and down mouse-holes. They are sprinkled all over the countryside, and it is the little animals, and particularly the birds, who know where they are.

And so if a squirrel knew where there was a nickel, it was worth his trouble to bring it along with his winter supply of nuts to the bank. For five months his hoard would be safe from the robbers against whom he must be always on the watch.

But there were many other things besides nuts brought in for safekeeping. Oddly enough, the three wealthiest depositors in the bank were Ferdinand, the crow, and Alice and Emma, the two ducks. Ferdinand, like all crows, was a great collector. In his nest in the dead pine over in the woods he was popularly supposed to have hidden a treasure worth a king's ransom. Indeed, there were some valuable things in his collection—half a dozen gold coins, a brooch set with diamonds in the form of a rabbit, a number of unmounted emeralds and sapphires, and so on. But Ferdinand collected things that were bright and glittered, regardless of their value, and so mixed in with these things which men, too, like to hoard, there were bits of glass and shiny bottle-caps and pins and pieces of tin and a brass thimble. All these things Ferdinand brought into the bank for safekeeping, for lately he had noticed a number of blue jays hanging around the pine tree, and blue jays are great thieves.

Alice and Emma didn't care much about collecting, although in exploring the mud in the bottoms of ponds and creeks they often picked up things that had been dropped out of boats. But they had inherited their Uncle Wesley's collection, and that was a very fine collection indeed. For Uncle Wesley had traveled a great deal and had stirred up the mud at the bottom of many much-traveled lakes and streams and had found and brought home more jewelry than you could shake a stick at. Alice and Emma kept the collection at the bottom of Mr. Bean's duck pond, but they were nervous, fluttery little ducks and were always worrying about it. Emma didn't care for jewelry and never wore any, but Alice occasionally put on a string of pearls when she went calling. She would have liked to wear some of the diamonds, but Emma did not think that diamonds were refined. The ducks were very much relieved when they had entrusted all this wealth to the bank.

One day when the bank had been open about a week Mr. Bean harnessed Hank, the old white horse, to the buggy and started into town. But when he came opposite the shed, with the big sign in front, he pulled on the reins. "Whoa, Hank," he shouted. "What in tarnation's this?"

Hank looked around but didn't say anything. Mr. Bean knew that his animals could talk, but he was a pretty conventional man. That means that he didn't like new things very much. He liked to have everything go on as it had when he was a boy. That was the reason he still drove a buggy instead of a car. And so it made him feel uncomfortable and a little embarrassed when he heard animals talk. He just couldn't get used to it.

It was a little confusing for the animals sometimes. Mr. Bean thought them impolite if they didn't answer, and, on the other hand, it upset him if they did. But in this case Hank decided that no answer was necessary.

If Mr. Bean wanted to know what the bank was, he only had to read the sign.

Which he did. "First Animal Bank, hey?" he said. "So that's what they've started. Good, sound idea. Teach 'em the value of money. 'President: John Quincy Adams—' Hey, hey; we can't have this! You animals'll be getting me into trouble with the government—using that name. Tut, tut; we'll have to see about this!" And he dropped the reins on the dashboard and climbed out.

He walked into the shed and up to the counter that the two boys, Byram and Adoniram, had built for the bankers. A horse with a straw hat on who had come in to inquire if the bank would lend him the money to buy a new pair of shoes moved aside respectfully, and John Quincy, who had been talking to the horse, hopped forward.

"Good morning, sir," he said. "What can we do for you?"

Mr. Bean gave a slight shudder, as he always did when he heard an animal speak. "Who are you?" he said. "Stranger here, ain't you?"

"Not any longer, I hope, sir," said the woodpecker. "Let us say, rather, a new arrival in your delightful community."

"This is John Quincy, Mr. Bean," said Jinx. "The president of our new bank."

Mr. Bean gave a grunt. Then he said: "Well, if his name's John Quincy, his name's John Quincy. If he's president of the bank, he's president of the bank. But you got to take that name Adams off your sign."

"But that's his name," protested Jinx. "He was named after the President."

"I was named after my grandfather," said Mr. Bean, "but I don't go round pretending I'm him."

"Neither do I," said the woodpecker indignantly.

"Go round pretending you're my grandfather?" said Mr. Bean. "I should hope not."

"Go round pretending I'm the President," said John Quincy.

"Oh," said Mr. Bean. "Well, maybe you don't. But it looks like it. And whether you are or not, folks are going to criticize me for letting you do it. So fix up that sign."

He turned to go, but the horse with the straw hat said nervously: "Don't you—don't you approve of this bank, Mr. Bean? Don't you think it's a good bank?"

"Approve of it? Certainly I approve of it. It's the first animal bank in the country, ain't it? It's run by

• • • Good morning, sir. What can we do for you? • • •

my animals, ain't it? That is, all but this John Quincy, here, and I expect he's all right. Who says it ain't a good bank?"

"Why, n-nobody," said the horse.

"Well, then," said Mr. Bean. He looked sharply at the horse. "I've seen you before somewhere," he said.

"I'm Zenas Witherspoon's Jerry," said the horse. "I just came over to see if I could borrow enough to buy some new shoes."

"Oh, sure. I thought I recognized that long nose," said Mr. Bean. "Why don't Zenas buy shoes for you?"

"He hasn't any money. He had a bad year last year."

"Well," said Mr. Bean, "he hadn't ought to bought you that hat. In my day horses didn't wear hats. They weren't afraid of a little sun."

"It's Mrs. Witherspoon's hat," said Jerry. "She don't ever go out, so she gave it to me."

" 'Twa'n't much of a present," said Mr. Bean dryly. Then he said to John Quincy: "Well, president, what you going to do about this loan? I want to see how your bank works."

"We can't lend you our depositors' money unless you can give us good security," said John Quincy. "I guess we'll have to refuse the loan."

"Security," said Jerry. "What's that?"

"It's anything of value that you'd leave with us. Then if you couldn't pay back the money when you'd promised to, we'd sell the thing and get our money."

"Or maybe you could get somebody to go on your note," suggested Freddy.

"Gosh," said the horse perplexedly, "you certainly have a lot of ways of saying that you won't lend me the money."

"He just means you might get somebody to promise to pay back the money if you can't yourself," said Jinx.

The horse dropped his head. "There ain't anybody," he said sadly. "I guess I'll just have to try to do the spring plowing in my bare hoofs." And he turned to go.

"I'll go on your note," said Mr. Bean suddenly. "Give him the money, Jinx, and I'll sign the paper. I suppose I'll lose out on it and old Zenas'll laugh his head off at my buying shoes for his horse, but I can't see an animal put on that way—even somebody else's animal."

So they gave Jerry six dollars and he thanked Mr. Bean and galloped off to the blacksmith shop, Mrs.

37

Witherspoon's hat cocked gaily over his right ear.

"What's more," said Mr. Bean, "I guess I'd better make a little deposit in the First Animal myself." And he drew out a roll of bills and peeled off a hundred dollars and opened an account with it. Then he went out and got in the buggy and picked up the reins and said: "Giddap!"

When Mr. Bean got to town he went first into the First National Bank of Centerboro, which was an imposing white marble structure on the corner of Main and Liberty Streets. He went into the handsome office of the president, Mr. Henry Weezer, and sat down.

"Well, Henry," he said, "you've got some competition out our way."

Mr. Weezer was a small neat man with white hair, starched cuffs, and gold-rimmed nose glasses that fell off whenever you mentioned a sum of money larger than ten dollars.

"Yes, sir," said Mr. Bean, "don't my animals beat all? They've opened a bank."

"Dear me," said Mr. Weezer in a dry voice. He didn't smile, but Mr. Bean didn't mind, because Mr. Weezer never smiled unless you paid him something. He was not an unkind man, though—just terribly interested in banking.

"Yes, sir," said Mr. Bean, "a regular bank. And they've got safe-deposit vaults that no burglar could ever get into."

"You don't tell me," said Mr. Weezer.

"I do tell you," said Mr. Bean, "and furthermore I tell you that they're the smartest animals in the country. I was kind of hesitating about taking that trip abroad together with Mrs. Bean and the boys though Mrs. Bean has her heart so set on it; but my land! animals that can run a regular bank can certainly look after a farm for half a year."

"I should think they could," admitted Mr. Weezer. "Well, I'll try to bear up under the competition. I expect they won't cut into our business a great deal."

"Don't ye be too sure," said Mr. Bean. "They've got deposits now of $179.42."

Mr. Weezer's glasses fell off, but he put them on again hurriedly and looked sharply at Mr. Bean. "What!" he exclaimed. "Animals have put that much money in a bank?"

"Animals and folks. They've got at least one man as depositor, I know."

"Oh, but look here," said Mr. Weezer excitedly, "they can't do that, Mr. Bean. This is a real bank you're talking about. There isn't room for two real banks in Centerboro. Oh, dear me, I must ask you to stop it at once."

"Now hold your horses, Henry," said Mr. Bean. "If my animals want to start a bank, they can start a bank. They got as good a right as you have."

"They have no right to cut into our business here," said Mr. Weezer angrily. "I won't have it! I'll take it up with the authorities—"

Mr. Bean got up. "Stuff and nonsense!" he said. "I thought you'd like the idea, Henry. Smart animals. Credit to the town."

But Mr. Weezer didn't feel that way about it at all. He said again that he was going to complain to the authorities, and he picked up the telephone and called the authorities up. But Mr. Bean got mad, and he walked out to the cashier's window and drew out all his money, which amounted to $4,845.92 and he drove back and deposited it in the First Animal.

So at the end of that day the deposits of the First Animal Bank of Centerboro came to a grand total of $5,025.44 as you can figure out for yourself. Only you won't come out right unless you remember that while Mr. Bean was in town a rabbit had brought in a dime to deposit.

IV

On the other side of the stone wall that divided the orchard from the back pasture stood an old gnarled apple tree. There was a hole in the trunk right by the ground, and in it lived a fox named John.

John was one of the woods animals who had come down to live on the farm because they wanted to take part in the gay social life of the farm animals. A great many squirrels had moved down, and several porcupines and coons, and even Peter, the bear, often came down for a week when there was something special going on. When John had first moved into the apple tree, Charles, the rooster, and his wife, Henrietta, had been very much upset. For there is nothing that a fox would rather have for supper than a nice plump chicken. Unless it is two plump chickens. But a committee, consisting of Robert and Mrs. Wiggins, had called on John and made him promise to leave the chickens alone. John promised readily enough, for he liked society, and there wasn't much of that up in the wild and lonely woods. And anyway he didn't specially care for chicken. What he really liked was duck. But he didn't tell the committee that.

The hole in the apple tree was pretty small. It was so small that John could just get himself in when he curled up tight. And even then he had to leave his bushy tail outside. But he didn't mind. "For," he said, "I'm not in it very much. I spend most of my time outdoors when I'm awake. All I really need is a place to sleep."

One afternoon Freddy left the bank early and trotted off down through the orchard. He sprang over the wall as lightly as a cat. For although Freddy was getting fat, he exercised regularly and, like many fat people, was very light on his feet. He was a wonderful dancer.

As he walked toward the apple tree he paused to admire the cloud effects, and he murmured a verse or two of poetry to himself. Like most pigs, he was extremely artistic. He often felt that he might have been a great painter if he had only had time to turn his hand to it. "A lovely bank of clouds," he said to himself as he moved on, and then he shook his head crossly. "Now, why did I say 'bank'! Good gracious, can't I get my mind off business for a second?"

When he came to the tree he saw a reddish, bushy tail sticking out of the hole, and he was about to knock when he noticed a small sign tied to the end of the tail. The sign said: "Out."

"Oh, dear," said Freddy, "now I'll have to come back again this evening." And he was about to turn away when the tail was whisked in and then pushed out again immediately with another sign on it which said: "In."

So Freddy knocked on the tree.

The tail was withdrawn again and John's sharp little nose poked out. "Why, Freddy," said the fox, "this is a pleasant surprise. Come in, come in! No, just a minute. I have to come out first." For his house was so small that if he wanted to entertain anybody in it he had to sit outside himself.

"Let's just sit out here together," said the pig.

So they sat down under the apple tree, which was covered with white blossoms, and Freddy said: "Why

43

the signs, John? I could see you were in, with your tail sticking out in plain sight."

"That's just the trouble," said the fox. "It's the only drawback to this house. Of course I'm always in to you, Freddy, when you come to call, but there are some animals that come—well, I name no names. But you know how it is—they just never go *home*. Now if I had a regular-sized house, I just wouldn't answer when they knocked, or my butler would go and tell them I was not at home. But when they can *see* me—well, I thought if I had the signs made, then when they saw it read: 'Out,' they'd understand I wasn't seeing anybody and go away."

"Does it work?" asked Freddy.

"No. That is, with some of the more polite ones it does. But there are some— Why, that skunk, Sniffy Wilson, came yesterday. I had the 'Out' sign on my tail. But do you think he went away? He did not. He actually pulled my tail until I answered him. Said he thought it was a doorbell. Some people simply don't know how to behave, Freddy; that's all there is about it."

"Sniffy's kind of free and easy, and that's a fact," said Freddy. "But he's a good fellow—always willing to help you out if you're in a jam. Well, that's one

· · · The sign said OUT · · ·

reason I came over to see you today. We're in sort of a jam at the bank. We've got to have some more vaults built, and this time it's a job for highly skilled labor—it's no woodchuck proposition. The rooms are full now, and even the tunnel is so cluttered up with stuff that the clerks can hardly get through. You're just the animal for the job, if you'll take it."

Freddy was very diplomatic. He knew how to make people want to do the things he wanted them to do. John felt very much flattered, and he agreed at once to come and do the necessary digging. So they gossiped for a while and then John said:

"There's some talk up in the woods, Freddy, that you've given up the idea of founding a republic and electing a president. I hope that isn't so."

"No," said Freddy, and he explained that they had merely taken John Quincy's advice about getting the bank going first. "It's sound advice, I think," said the pig. "Once we start having election speeches and going out after votes, nobody is going to pay much attention to the bank. But I think we will get at it pretty soon now."

"Well, I hope so," said the fox. "And of course it's none of my business—well, in a way it is, of course, because I'm a citizen of the republic, if there is a republic, and—well—"

"Well, go ahead," said Freddy. "You're among friends."

"Well," said John, "I wouldn't take too much wood-pecker advice, if I were you. I don't trust those boys, and that's a fact. Don't ask me why. It's just a feeling. Don't you have those feelings?"

"Why, now you mention it," said Freddy, "I guess I do. Weasels, now. I don't trust weasels. And yet I haven't any reason not to, really. I don't know much about them. They may be the kindest, nicest people in the world. But somehow—"

"Yes," said John. "That's how I feel about wood-peckers. Well, anyway, I just thought I'd mention it."

"Glad you did," said Freddy. "Glad you did. I'll keep it in mind. Well, I guess I must be getting back."

So he said good-by, and John hung the "Out" sign on the end of his tail and crawled back into his house and took a nap.

When Freddy got back to the bank, Jinx, who had not been in all day, was still not there, and John Quincy was very much upset. "We've got to do something about Jinx, Freddy," he said. "He's supposed to be here from ten to three, just like the rest of us. But sometimes he doesn't come in for days at a time."

Freddy's ears turned pink, for he had not been **any** too punctual himself. He seldom got up before ten o'clock in the morning, and by the time he had done his exercises and had a leisurely breakfast and worked awhile at his poetry and at his plans for the election, it was time for dinner, and then after dinner there was his nap, and various other things to be seen to, so that he often didn't get to the bank before half past two. And the bank closed at three.

"Oh, well," he said, "we mustn't be too hard on Jinx. After all, there's always somebody here—"

"There's always *me* here," said John Quincy. "Not that I mind the extra work, but it's the principle of the thing. Ten to three; those are our hours. And we're all supposed to be here.—Ah, here he is now," he said, as Jinx poked his head in the door.

"Hi, gents," said the cat breezily. "Boy, what a day! What a day I've had! Ah, spring, spring! I made a poem about it, Freddy.

Hooray for the spring! What a glorious feeling!
All the little lambs on the hillsides squealing!
Tighten up your braces! Tuck in your shirt!
All the little green things growing in the dirt!

I didn't really see any lambs, though. Spent most of the day chasing butterflies. Ah, what is more uplifting, my friends, than to sally forth in the glorious springtide and chase butterflies across the hills of Bean!"

"Indeed!" said John Quincy dryly. "And while you have been enjoying the spring, I have been slaving here in a stuffy office."

"The more fool you," said Jinx. "Anyway, you like to slave and stuff, doesn't he, Freddy?"

"Please leave me out of it," said Freddy nervously, for John Quincy was beginning to tap nervously on the counter with his beak—a sure sign with woodpeckers that there is going to be a row.

"That is not the point," said John Quincy, suddenly raising his voice. "As an officer of this bank, it is your plain duty to be here in banking hours. Suppose Mr. Bean comes in and wants to talk to the treasurer and I have to tell him the treasurer's out chasing butterflies! What kind of a bank is that? We've had quite enough of this, Jinx. As president of this bank and your superior officer—"

"As president of this bank and my superior officer," interrupted Jinx, "you go soak your head in a rain barrel. You're right, we've had enough of it. I'm through. I started this bank to have some fun, not to be a woodpecker's slave. I quit, do you hear? I resign." And with a swipe of his paw he knocked John Quincy off the counter, and leaped out of the door.

"I'm sorry, J. Q.," said Freddy as the woodpecker picked himself up and smoothed down his feathers, "but you asked for it. That's no way to handle Jinx. He's a good fellow, but—"

"There's only one way to handle animals like him," said John Quincy, "and that's with a firm hand."

"I should say that Jinx was the one that used the firm hand," remarked the pig. "However, we're out a treasurer. And we'll have to have one. Who do you suggest?"

They talked for a time about possible candidates for the office of treasurer, but they might as well have saved their breath, for, as they soon found out, none of the animals on the farm wanted the job. Most of them, the dogs and the cows and Hank, the old white horse, had their regular jobs on the farm, so that they could not possibly work at banking from ten to three, and the others were hardly fitted for such a responsible position. And indeed the only one who really wanted to be treasurer was Charles, the rooster. Charles was rather pompous and was much esteemed as a public speaker—by everyone, that is, but his wife, Henrietta —and would in some ways have made a good bank treasurer. But his judgment wasn't very good, and that is a grave fault in either a rooster or a treasurer. So Freddy and John Quincy both said no.

"We've got to do something, though," said John Quincy. "We can't do business without a treasurer. Now I've been thinking it over, and if it's agreeable to you, I'll fly down to Washington over the week-end and have a talk with Father. I think perhaps I could persuade him to come up and take charge. He likes good food, Father does, and I will say that the bugs in New York State are the finest I've ever tasted."

"Well," said Freddy. "I must say I don't see why you and I can't run the bank. After all, there are days and days when nobody comes in at all."

"And there are days when somebody like Mr. Bean comes in," said John Quincy, "and what's he going to think if we say there isn't any treasurer? Is he going to put his money in a bank that isn't properly run?"

"I suppose not," said Freddy. "And, my gracious, it would be awful if he decided that we couldn't run a bank properly. He'd think we couldn't run the farm, and then he wouldn't take that trip abroad. And Mrs. Bean has been counting on it so."

"Don't you worry," said John Quincy. "We can run the farm all right. We'll get at this election pretty soon and fix the whole thing up."

"We?" said Freddy to himself as he bent over his ledger. "Somehow I don't like that 'we' so much."

V

Early Monday morning Freddy was awakened by a noise. It was so loud and so startling that he leaped out of bed and was half-way to the window before he had opened his eyes. He pulled aside the curtain and stared out, gasping with fright. But there was nothing there. Nothing, that is, but the big red barns and the little white house and the empty barnyard with the long early morning shadows across it. "Oh, my goodness!" he groaned.

And a voice said: "Good morning."

Freddy swung around. In the doorway stood Charles. "Do I wake 'em up or do I wake 'em up?"

said the rooster, and began drawing in his breath for another crow.

"No, no," said Freddy. "Stop it! I asked you to wake me up, not to blow me out of bed. And, my goodness, what time is it?"

"Just after five."

"Just after five! I asked you to wake me up early so I could get to the bank on time. But, good gracious, I don't want to get up in the middle of the night."

"You asked me to wake you early and I did," said Charles huffily. "Well, that's the thanks I get—doing things for people." He turned away grumbling, but Freddy said:

"Oh, forget it, Charles. We've got different ideas about what's early, that's all. Come in. Come in, and I'll—I'll show you my bicycle."

"Your what?" said Charles, forgetting his anger.

"Bicycle," said Freddy. "It used to belong to Mr. Bean. My legs were too short to reach the pedals, but Uncle Ben fixed them for me."

"How'd he do it? Stretch 'em?" asked Charles seriously.

"No, no," said Freddy. "I mean he fixed the pedals."

Uncle Ben was Mr. Bean's uncle, who had lived for a time at the farm. He was a fine mechanic, and it was he who had made the **clockwork** boy as a playmate for Adoniram.

Freddy went into his study and came out wheeling the bicycle. It was a real bicycle, all right, though pretty rusty, and the pedals had been moved higher up so that Freddy could reach them.

"I've never practiced riding it much," Freddy said. "Except that time I went into the pond. That's when it got so rusty. And I don't know when I'll get a chance now, with the bank business and election coming on. But it's a fine machine."

"Beautiful," said Charles, walking around and admiring it with his head on one side. "Look, Freddy, you've got five hours now you don't know what to do with. I expect it's too early in the morning for you to write any poetry. Why don't you practice riding now?"

"That's an idea," said the pig. He wheeled the bicycle out of the door. "Come on, Charles. Get up on the handlebars and I'll give you a ride."

"No, thanks," said the rooster. His judgment wasn't awfully good, but it was good enough to keep him off any bicycle that Freddy was riding.

"Well," said Freddy, "here goes." But he didn't seem very anxious to start. He stepped inside the frame and put one foot on the pedal and made a hop, but it was a very small hop, and the bicycle only moved forward about an inch. Then he stopped and looked up at the sky. "Wonder if it's going to rain," he said. "I wouldn't want to be caught miles from home in a rainstorm."

"There isn't a cloud in the sky," said Charles. "Come on, Freddy, do your stuff. Vault into the saddle and away. Don't get on like a girl."

Freddy bent over and spun the pedal. "I think these pedals need oiling," he said. And he leaned the bicycle against the wall and went in and got an oilcan and oiled the pedal. Then he oiled the other pedal. Then he oiled the handlebars. Then he turned the bicycle upside down and gave it a thorough oiling all over. Then he got a rag and polished it all over.

"If you have nice things, you ought to take proper care of them, I always say," he said. "I never start out unless I know my machine is in A-1, first-class condition. It pays in the end to take a little trouble about it. And while I'm at it, I'll just tighten things up a bit." And he went back in and got a wrench and tightened all the nuts, and then he got the pump and blew some more air into the tires. "Many a trip has been spoiled because of the lack of just some little thing," he said.

"Just a drop of oil may make all the difference between success and failure. Suppose Lindbergh hadn't oiled his machine before he started across the ocean that time. Where'd he be now?"

"Yeah," said Charles. "Suppose Lincoln hadn't oiled his horse before riding off to Gettysburg. Would he have won that battle?"

"Lincoln wasn't at the battle of Gettysburg," said Freddy.

"He was so," said Charles. "Hey, don't put any more oil on that thing. You aren't making a salad."

"He was not," said Freddy. "Come in and we'll look it up in the encyclopedia."

So they went into his study to look it up. The study was not very tidy, and they couldn't find the L volume of the encyclopedia at all. "Oh, I remember," said Freddy. "I lent it to Mrs. Bean because she wanted to look up a recipe for lamb stew. Mr. Bean doesn't like the kind she makes."

They found the G volume finally, although they had to hunt for a long time, for Freddy had used it to prop up one corner of his bed. And then they looked up Gettysburg, and Freddy proved to Charles that Lincoln had not attended the battle.

By that time it was half past seven.

"While we're in here," said Freddy, "I'd like to show you my stamp collection."

"I'm afraid that would be taking too much of your time," said Charles. "If you're going to practice riding your bicycle—"

"Oh, that's all right," said Freddy. "Lots of time. See here." He pulled out an old envelope from among some papers and shook out some stamps. There were only seventeen stamps, and eight of them were alike—just ordinary three-cent stamps torn from envelopes.

"Very interesting," said Charles. "But not what you'd call a really large collection."

"It is," said Freddy, "and it isn't. I suppose a collector like Adoniram wouldn't think much of it. He has over three thousand different kinds. But just the same I'm willing to bet it's the largest private stamp collection owned solely and exclusively by a pig. I bet there isn't a pig in the world that has got a bigger one."

"I bet there isn't a pig in the world that cares," said Charles. "And what's more, I bet there isn't another pig in the world but you that could think up so many things to keep from riding a bicycle."

"Why, what do you mean?" said Freddy indignantly. "Do you think I'm afraid to ride it?"

Charles didn't say anything. He just looked hard at Freddy with his left eye, and with his right eye he looked out of the window at the bicycle. And this was not as hard for him to do as you might think, for a rooster's eyes aren't set in the front of his head like yours, but are placed one on each side, so that it is no trouble at all for him to see what is going on in two places at once. Some people think that is why roosters, and hens too of course, seem to show such a lack of decision in a simple thing like crossing the road. They can't make up their minds which eye to rely on.

"Huh!" said Freddy. "I'll show you!" And he walked very boldly and resolutely out of the door and up to the bicycle, with an expression on his face like an early Christian martyr walking into the lions' den and glad to get it over.

He started to take hold of the handlebars and then he saw the oil-can. "Must take this in first," he said. And then he said: "My goodness, that reminds me! I haven't oiled Bertram this week. Gosh, I must do that right away."

Now, maybe you know about Bertram, and if you do, you can skip this paragraph. When Adoniram had first come to the farm, the animals thought it was too bad that he didn't have any other boy to play with.

So they got Uncle Ben to make a wooden boy who ran by clockwork. His name was Bertram and he could do almost everything a real boy can except think. Of course there had to be an engineer to run him, and Ronald, the rooster who had come to the farm with Adoniram, was chosen because he was small. There was a door in Bertram's back for Ronald to get in by, and a little window in Bertram's chest for him to look out of, and inside there was a perch facing all the levers that controlled Bertram's arms and legs. There was even a microphone fixed up so that Ronald could talk for him. He was a good deal more complicated to run than an automobile, but Ronald got on to it very quickly, and Adoniram and Bertram (his clockwork twin) had many fine times together.

But when the other boy, Byram, came, Bertram wasn't much use any more, since Adoniram didn't need a clockwork playmate any longer; so now he had sat for weeks and months upstairs in the barn in Uncle Ben's old workshop. When they had parties or parades, either Ronald or one of the small animals who had learned to run Bertram would take him out, so it was Freddy's duty to see that he was always oiled and wound up and ready to go.

Charles was the only one who was never allowed to run Bertram. At least he was never allowed to if any of the other animals could stop him before he got inside. Once he was in, however, and had set the machinery going, it was no use trying to stop him, for Bertram was tremendously strong.

Charles didn't mean to do any harm when he took Bertram out; all he really wanted to do was to turn up the microphone as high as it would go and then make long speeches, which could be heard for miles. He just liked the sound of his own voice, and the louder it was, the better he liked it. But he wasn't very smart about machinery, and when he was inside Bertram and making a speech, he got so excited that he pulled all the levers and handles at once, and then Bertram either would get his arms and legs all tied up in a knot or else would begin to smash things, and once during a Fourth of July oration his head went round and round like a top, faster and faster, until finally it flew off and went through Mr. Bean's front parlor window and knocked over a whatnot on which were a pink china cat, and a bottle with a ship inside it, and another bottle with "Mother" painted on it surrounded by a wreath of nasturtiums, and a photograph of Mrs. Bean in a frame covered with shells, and other bric-a-brac. And that kind of thing was dangerous, for though Bertram's head was wood and weighed fifteen pounds, it wouldn't stand much of that kind of treatment.

So when Freddy said he must go oil Bertram, Charles forgot all about the bicycle. Of course it would be fun to see Freddy fall off the bicycle, but it would be more fun to run Bertram, if Freddy would let him. So they went up to the workshop.

There was Bertram sitting on the floor in a corner with an old horse blanket over his head to keep off the dust.

"He looks like Sitting Bull at the council fire," said Freddy.

"Oh, look, Freddy," said Charles. "Let's play he is an Indian. Dress him up in feathers and things and I'll get in him and—"

"No," said Freddy.

"Aw, come on," Charles pleaded. "I won't take him out of the barnyard. Honest, Freddy. Listen, I won't even take him out of the barn."

"No!" said Freddy. "I know as well as you do that you can make a speech that can be heard over half the county without going outside the barn. And even if I could trust you not to do something awful, I wouldn't let you run him now, when Mr. Bean is so worried about whether we're responsible enough to run the farm while he's away."

"Well, he thinks I'm responsible even if you don't," said Charles. "Just the other day we were all sitting on the fence by the First Animal when he and Mrs. Bean came back from town. He'd been down to get his steamship tickets. And as soon as I saw him, I cautioned 'em all—I said: 'Hey, boys, look responsible now.' So we all sat there looking responsible, and he pulled up and sat there looking at us, and then he said: 'My, my! they all look so solemn; I wonder if it's because we're going away, Mrs. B.?' And Mrs. Bean said: 'They all look like they got stomach-aches to me, Mr. B.' And Mr. Bean said: 'That there rooster—he's the worst. He looks like he aches all over.' Then Mrs. Bean said she guessed she'd better brew a cup of her boneset tea for me, and Mr. Bean said: 'That'll change his expression some, anyway.' And they sat there laughing and giggling for a while, and then drove on."

"I wouldn't think that was looking responsible," said Freddy. "Looking as if you had a stomach-ache."

"Oh, is that so? Well, how would you do it?"

"Oh, I'd look sort of serious and solemn, as if I had

something on my mind."

"Well, that's how I feel when I've got the stomach-ache. I don't go round kicking up my heels and grinning. Look, Freddy, let me oil part of him, will you?"

Freddy was a good executive: that is, he never liked to do any work he could get anyone else to do for him. So he said: "All right. But no funny business," and handed over the oil-can. Charles didn't understand the oil-can very well, and he got a lot of oil on his feathers. But he worked away under Freddy's direction and got Bertram's shoulders and neck and wrists and elbows oiled up. And then suddenly he gave a squawk and said: "Oh, look, Freddy! Look at the window!" And as Freddy turned to look, Charles pulled open the little door in Bertram's back and jumped in and slammed it behind him.

"Hey!" shouted Freddy. "Hey! Get out of there, you ninny! You've got no business—"

"Ha ha!" boomed Charles's voice, magnified a hundred times by the microphone. "I'll show you who's a ninny!" And he began pulling at the levers that set Bertram in motion, and Bertram got up and began whirling his arms around. And then as Freddy ducked hastily under Uncle Ben's work-bench, Bertram made three jumps. The first jump took him into the middle of the room, and the second jump took him to the head of the stairs, and the third took him right down the stairs, and there was a terrible crashing and banging and bumping. "Oh dear, oh dear!" said Freddy, and dashed down the stairs; and there was Bertram lying on his face on the floor, and his left arm was around his own neck and his left leg was hanging all by itself over the handle of a wheelbarrow.

When Freddy got to him, Charles was trying to get Bertram to stand up. But with one leg off he couldn't manage it. And so he decided to have Bertram make his speech anyway, even if he was lying flat on his face. "Ladies and gentlemen," he began, "the position in which you find me today is not, I admit, the one in which I should have chosen to address you. But it is not for nothing that I have been called Charles the Fearless, Charles the Imperturbable." And then he stopped. For something had happened to the microphone, and no sound came out of Bertram at all. So he opened the little door and hopped out.

"All right, all right," he said impatiently to Freddy, who was calling on him frantically to come out. "Here I am."

"Yes, here you are!" said Freddy bitterly. "And what good has that ever been to anybody? Responsible Charles—that's you!—Say, wait a minute. What was that word you used? The one you said they called you?"

Freddy, being a poet, was always interested in new words which he could work into his poems, and he suddenly forgot all about scolding Charles. So Charles told him what the word meant and Freddy made a note of it, and then Freddy said: "Look here, if Mr. Bean sees Bertram in this state, he's going to be pretty upset. We'll have to get the boys to carry him upstairs and put him together again."

So Charles went out and found Byram and Adoniram, and they carried Bertram and his leg upstairs and started to put them together.

"See here, Charles," said Freddy, "I'm not going to say any more about this, but the other animals are going to be pretty sore. Now, if I were you—"

"If you were me," interrupted Charles, "you could stay here and talk some more. But as it is, you have to get to the bank. It's almost ten o'clock."

"What!" said Freddy. "Good gracious, and to-day's the day John Quincy and his father get back, and we have to have a board meeting. I'll have to run."

"Take your bicycle," said Charles.

Freddy hesitated. "I suppose it would be quicker," he said.

"Sure," said the rooster. "Just through the barnyard and then coast down the hill to the bank.—Unless, of course, you're afraid?"

Freddy looked at him a minute. "Certainly I'm not afraid!" he said crossly. He picked up the bicycle, looking this time like an early Christian martyr out of whom the lions have already taken two or three bites. He put a foot on the pedal, gave a couple of skips, and was off.

Not off the bicycle, although he came pretty near it as he grazed the corner of the pigpen. But off through the barnyard, and out of the gate, and then whizzing faster and faster down the hill until Charles lost sight of him. "Responsible!" said the rooster. "Responsible your grandmother's tail-feathers!"

And even as he spoke, Freddy was getting off the bicycle. He got off much more quickly than he intended to. For even before he left the barnyard the bicycle was going much faster than was really enjoyable. But he didn't know how to stop it. He had forgotten about the brake. So he kept pedaling faster and faster until his fat little legs were just a blur; and

• • • through the window of the First Animal Bank • • •

the bicycle responded nobly, and down the hill it went at forty miles an hour, which is high speed on a bicycle, though not much in an aeroplane.

But it seemed very much like an aeroplane to Freddy. And he was just thinking: "Oh dear, oh dear, I suppose flying is like this, and I guess I don't ever want to fly," when the bicycle hit a stone, bounced, went into a ditch, over the ditch, and whang into a stone wall. And for a minute Freddy really was flying. Very gracefully he sailed over the wall and through the window of the First Animal Bank of Centerboro. And landed with a terrible crash in the president's office.

Freddy was sort of dazed for a minute, but he was pretty fat and the fall hadn't hurt him much. He was aware of a lot of squawking and fluttering, and some feathers tickling his nose. And then he got up. Three woodpeckers were sitting on the edge of the counter, shaking themselves and settling their feathers.

"Well, John Quincy," said the oldest woodpecker, "who, may I ask, is this rather impetuous gentleman?"

"This?" said John Quincy. "Oh, yes, Father. This is our distinguished secretary. On time, for the first time in his banking career, too. It is exactly ten o'clock. We are thankful to be still alive to congratulate you, Freddy."

VI

Freddy was pretty embarrassed. To arrive at an important banking conference on time was the proper thing to do, of course; but to arrive flying through the window, and knocking all the other bankers flat on the floor, was a little unusual. It would hardly impress anybody with his responsibility. And yet he *had* been on time. He decided, very wisely, to stick to that point and not to apologize too much. After all, nobody had been injured.

"I'm sorry if I startled you," he said. "But I was anxious to be punctual."

"I'm glad you didn't try to get here early," said John Quincy sarcastically. "Let me introduce you.

This is my father, Grover, and my son, X."

"X?" said Freddy. "Really? I never heard that name before."

"Well, you see," said John Quincy, "we're always named after the presidents, but we're a pretty large family now, and we have used up all the names, so until a new president is elected we haven't a name for him. So we just call him X.—And now should we get to business? I should tell you, Freddy, that my father feels that it would hardly be dignified for him to take Jinx's place as treasurer and work under me as president. So we have decided to make him president, and I will be treasurer."

"Why, I guess that's all right," said Freddy.

"Very well," said John Quincy. "Shall we put it to a vote? I move that John Quincy be made treasurer, and Grover president, of the First Animal Bank."

"I second the motion," said Freddy.

"Motion made and seconded," said John Quincy. "All in favor say 'Aye.'"

So he and Freddy said: "Aye."

"Motion passed," said John Quincy. "Now is there any other business?" And then he stopped, for there was a tap on the door and John came in.

"Morning, gentlemen," said the fox. "I just dropped

in to see if the new vaults were satisfactory. That was some digging! Boy! Struck a flat rock as big as a barn. But I got around and under it finally and made a room as big as all the others together."

"Thank you," said John Quincy stiffly. "I have seen the vaults and they are quite satisfactory. But if you will excuse us—we are holding a board meeting, and—"

"Oh, sure, sure," said John. "Go right ahead. I'll just sit here in the corner till you're through."

"That's all right, John," said Freddy. "Well, J. Q., go ahead."

"Just a minute," said John Quincy. He came over and whispered in Freddy's ear. "We can't carry on a board meeting with outsiders present," he said. "I don't want to hurt your friend's feelings, but really—"

"There's nothing secret about this meeting," said Freddy. "And I'm certainly not going to tell him to leave."

John Quincy thought a minute. "Leave it to me," he said. Then he went back to his place. "Before continuing with the other business of the meeting," he said, "I would like to move that we use this fine large room in the vaults that John has made for us as the meeting place for the board. I move that it be known hereafter as the board room, and that all board meetings be held therein."

"That's a good idea," said Freddy. "I second the motion."

So they voted and passed it, and then John Quincy said: "Now we will go down to the board room and have our meeting." He motioned to the squirrel that was sitting on the plank that covered the entrance to the vaults, and the squirrel tugged the plank aside, and the three woodpeckers started down the tunnel.

"Hey, wait a minute!" said Freddy. "That tunnel's too small for me. I can't get into the board room."

"Dear me," said John Quincy, "we should have thought of that before we voted."

"But you can't hold a meeting without me," said the pig.

"You've had notice of the meeting and where it was to be," said John Quincy. "If you aren't there, the meeting goes on just the same."

"All right," said Freddy; "then I move we hold the meetings up here."

"You can't. Your motion has to be made at a meeting, and we've just passed the rule that all meetings have to be held in the board room. Come, Father! X!"

"Just a minute," said Freddy. "X can't go. He isn't a member of the board."

"Quite right," said John Quincy. "Xie, you stay here." And he and Grover disappeared down the tunnel.

"Well, what do you know about that?" said Freddy.

John looked at him and then at X, who was nonchalantly scratching his ear, and then he winked and went outside. In a minute Freddy followed him.

"Looks to me," said John, "as if your bank was being taken away from you."

"See if I care!" said Freddy. "We only started the thing for fun. If they want to run it, it's all right with me."

"Just the same," said the fox seriously, "it's got a lot of things that belong to Mr. Bean's animals in it now, to say nothing of Mr. Bean's own money. You don't want these outsiders running it."

"Oh, J. Q.'s all right," said Freddy. "He'll run it a lot better than we would. Still, I see your point. I'll talk to Jinx."

"And another thing," said John. "When are you going to start this republic and have the election?"

"The election?" said Freddy. "Oh, we thought in a week or so we could get at it. Now the bank's going."

74

"Well, don't put it off too long," said the fox. "Unless you want to have a woodpecker as president of the farm as well as of the bank."

"Why, what do you mean?" asked Freddy.

"Just this," said John. "You aren't around the bank much, you know, Freddy. But I've been working in the vaults, and I hear what's going on. I won't say I haven't tried to hear, for I was always suspicious of woodpeckers. Even when I was a little cub I didn't like them. Well, anyway, every customer that comes in, John Quincy starts in on him about what a lot of trouble there's going to be on the farm when Mr. Bean goes away unless we elect a pretty high-class president. Well, there's nothing wrong in that, but then he goes on to tell how much he and his father know about government, and how much experience they have had and so on. And then he says: 'Of course we are practically strangers in your beautiful community, and so we don't like to seem to criticize, particularly when everyone has been so kind to us. But do you really think that any of your good citizens are experienced enough to manage a big farm like this?'

"Well, of course, then the customer says: 'Well, maybe they're not.' And a lot of them have said that they wished we could have someone like John Quincy

75

or his father for president. Then John Quincy says: Oh, no, he didn't mean that! My goodness, no! He wouldn't *think* of trying to butt in and run for president. Well, you see what happens, Freddy. A lot of animals are getting the idea that one of these woodpeckers would make a pretty good president for us."

"Oh, pooh," said Freddy. "How many votes would he get on this farm? We'll all stand together and elect one of our own crowd. Only, maybe you're right. Everybody's been having so much fun with the bank that we've sort of let the election slide. Well, I'll get right at it."

"Good," said John. And he leaped up on the wall, ran along it a little way, and disappeared in the underbrush.

Freddy went into the bank. X was sitting in the same place, scratching his other ear. After a few minutes there was a tap on the plank and when the squirrel pulled it aside Grover and John Quincy came up.

"A very successful board meeting," said John Quincy. "Sorry you couldn't be with us, Freddy."

"Say, look here, you two," said Freddy. "You put something over on me about this board-room business all right. I admit it. I don't know what you got by it, but let me warn you: don't try to put anything over

· · · · Sorry you couldn't be with us · · · ·

on me a second time."

John Quincy blinked and looked at Grover, who ruffled up his feathers angrily and said: "Mr.–ah–Secretary, I resent the tone of that remark, both as president of this bank and as an honorable woodpecker. You yourself voted to have the new underground room used as a board room, and to have all board meetings held there. You were notified that a meeting was to be held. If you did not choose to attend that meeting, why blame us for it?"

"Listen," said Freddy. "You can argue a quart into a jelly glass. But I'm not arguing. I'm telling you. You think it over."

And he walked out and picked up his bicycle and wheeled it up the hill.

In the barnyard he met Charles and Ronald.

"For goodness' sake!" said Charles. "I thought you were half-way to Mexico by this time, the rate you were going down that hill. Have a nice ride?"

"Lovely," said Freddy. "Simply lovely. Wonderful what a feeling of freedom it gives you, bicycling. Almost like flying."

"And you didn't fall off?" asked Charles, looking a little disappointed.

"Fall off!" said Freddy. "Who–me? Don't be

funny! I simply flew. Had plenty of time. I—er—I dropped in on them just as they were starting the meeting. Dropped in—h'm, yes. I startled them a bit. By the way, Ronald, I've got an announcement to make. Come on over and get Bertram out."

Whenever any of the animals had an important announcement to make, he would tell Ronald what it was, and then the rooster would bring Bertram out into the barnyard and turn up the microphone so his voice could be heard all over the farm, and make the announcement. It was a pretty good arrangement, but at first the animals had used it so much that it had bothered Mr. Bean. And when one day Henrietta had used it to broadcast a full account of the wedding of one of her daughters, Calliope, to a young rooster from Taberg, with the names of the guests and a description of all the presents, he put his foot down. "For all the peace and quiet you get on this farm," he said, "you might as well be livin' down to the boiler works. If I want to hear a lot of yelling, I can turn on my radio. It's getting so I can't set down for a minute's comfort without expectin' to be lifted out of my chair by that dumb voice. Henceforth, you animals will confine yourselves to announcements that are really important, or I'll chop up Bertram for kindling and have Ronald fricasseed for Sunday dinner." So after that the animals were pretty careful what they broadcast.

Byram and Adoniram had got Bertram's leg back on when Freddy and Ronald came up the stairs. "I think you'd better get in him now, Ronald," said Byram, "and see if he works all right. We've done the best we can with him, but he was pretty well shaken up."

Bertram was shaken up all right. He could do all the things he had done before, but every now and then there would be a click and a buzz in his insides and then he would begin to act queer. He would hippety-hop, or swing his arms around like a windmill, and once he reached around and opened the door in his back and pulled Ronald's tail-feathers.

"I can't do anything with him when he does that," said the rooster. "But it's always when I try to work his right arm. I guess some of the wheels must have got mixed up when he fell downstairs."

"I wish Uncle Ben were here," said Adoniram. "He could fix him."

"Well, anyway, you can make my announcement," said Freddy.

So Bertram went down into the barnyard—he walked downstairs on his hands, which was pretty hard on Ronald, sitting on his perch in the little control room—and said in his loudest voice: "Hear ye! Hear ye!"

The voice boomed out over the woods and meadows and hills, and all over the farm animals came out of their holes, or looked up from their work or their munching or their hunting, and pointed their ears toward the barnyard.

"Announcement from Freddy," roared Bertram. "There will be a meeting tonight in the big barn to make plans for the formation of the first animal republic. Have your nominations for the presidency ready. Dancing after the meeting. Bring your own refreshments."

Mrs. Bean looked up from Mr. Bean's old carpet bag, which she was packing for the trip to Europe. "My land!" she exclaimed. "That Freddy is a card. What won't he be up to next! First a bank and now a republic. Did you know about this, Mr. B.?"

"*Oui, oui,*" said Mr. Bean, looking up from the book of French conversation he was studying. "That means 'yes' in French, Mrs. B., in case you don't know."

"Sakes alive, you talk it like a native, Mr. B.," said Mrs. Bean admiringly.

"*Oui, oui,*" said Mr. Bean again, proudly. "I guess

I got a gift for languages. Well, yes, Mrs. B., I heard something about this republic. Sensible thing. They want to elect a president and have a regular government and all, to run things while you and I and the boys are away. I've always said there wasn't no animals anywhere that could beat 'em for goodness and kindness—and smartness too. But now I say there ain't any can beat 'em for responsibility."

"Well," said Mrs. Bean, "they've had a good example set for them—that's why."

"Yes, I expect I have set 'em an example of responsibleness. But I know who's set 'em an example of goodness and kindness—and smartness too, Mrs. B."

"Get along with you," said Mrs. Bean, combing out the tassel of Mr. Bean's spare nightcap before tucking it into the bag. "Let me hear you say that in French."

So Mr. Bean began thumbing through his French book. But Jinx, who had been dozing on a clean calico dress in Mrs. Bean's suitcase under the bed, grinned to himself, then tiptoed out to report the conversation to Freddy.

VII

There wasn't much work done on the Bean farm
that afternoon, though there was a good deal of
activity. Animals hurried back and forth across the
barnyard and gathered in groups to talk and argue,
and there were even one or two fights among the
rougher element down by the creek on the edge of
the woods—the water rats and weasels. Freddy was a
little worried when he learned that the bank had closed
early and that the three woodpeckers were making a
nest-to-nest canvass of all the birds on the farm. "Fine

way to run our bank!" he said to himself. And he was
even more worried when he met old Simon, the rat,
and his son, Ezra, coming round the corner of the barn.
For the rats had not been seen in the barnyard for over
two years—not since the famous trial for murder in
which Freddy had so ably defended Jinx against the
false charge made by the rats of having killed and eaten
a crow.

Simon grinned wickedly at the pig.

"Ah, my clever friend," he said, "still a trifle over-
weight, are you not?"

"You'd better not let Jinx see you, Simon," said
Freddy, "or you'll lose a lot more weight than you can
afford to. What are you doing here, anyway? You're
not supposed to come up near the barn."

"As a free citizen of this new republic of yours, I
am exercising my rights," said the rat. "I presume you
won't deny us our votes?"

"No," said Freddy. "No. Though I'd like to."
And he hurried off to find Jinx.

He found him in the cow-barn, where Mrs. Wiggins, surrounded by a group of admiring friends, was
exhibiting a flag which she had designed for the new
republic. With a pair of old blue overalls and an old
white nightshirt and some old red flannel underwear

of Mr. Bean's which Georgie had begged for her from Mrs. Bean, she had laid out the flag, and then Adoniram had stitched it up for her on the sewing-machine. It was a good deal like the American flag, with two stars for Mr. and Mrs. Bean, and thirteen stripes for the thirteen original animals who had taken that famous first trip to Florida. There were also a number of buttonholes scattered about, which didn't stand for anything except that they hadn't been able to avoid them in cutting out the cloth.

"I have to laugh every time I look at those buttonholes," said Mrs. Wiggins. "What Mr. Bean will say when he sees his cast-off underwear flung to the breeze I'm sure I don't know."

"He'll be very proud and happy," said Robert.

"I was going to have Adoniram cut a couple of blue beans, instead of stars," said the cow. "But it did seem as if beans would be sort of funny on a flag. You can't imagine going into battle under a flag with beans on it."

"Personally, I can't imagine going into battle under any kind of a flag," said Freddy. "But I'm not very warlike. Anyway, I think it was very clever of you. I don't see how you ever thought of it."

"I don't know how anybody could help thinking of

85

it," said Mrs. Wiggins. "A country without a flag is as silly as a—as a— Well, I can't think of anything it's as silly as. As a pig without a tail, I guess, Freddy." She laughed her deep, comfortable laugh. "And as far as being clever goes—well, you know what they usually say about me. They say: 'That Mrs. Wiggins —she's got a heart of gold.' You notice they don't ever say anything about my head. Still, when you all say I'm clever, it wouldn't be polite to contradict you.— But what's on your mind, Freddy? I can always tell when something is worrying you by the way you keep grunting."

"I wasn't grunting," said Freddy. "I may have sighed once or twice—"

"It sounded like a grunt to me," said Mrs. Wiggins. "But, as I say, I'm not clever. Well, out with it."

"I just met Simon and Ezra out here," said Freddy. "And if you ask me, they're up to something."

"What!" said Jinx, jumping up. "You mean that they've dared to come into the barnyard? Why, wait till I get my paws on that old sneak-thief! I'll—"

"Hold on, hold on!" said Freddy. "You can't do that. Not until after election, anyway. As long as he behaves himself every animal that lives on this farm has a right to be at this meeting tonight, and to vote at

86

the election. And as far as we know, the rats have been behaving themselves for the last two years. But here's what's worrying me. We're the old crowd—the animals here in this cow-barn now. And as long as we stick together we won't have any trouble in electing the president we want, and running things the way Mr. Bean wants them run. But there are a lot of animals living on this farm that we don't ever have much to do with. Field mice, woodchucks, squirrels, chipmunks—and the birds. I dare say there are a hundred birds, and they all have votes. A good many of them will vote as we want them to. The squirrels will be with us. And I think I can guarantee the rabbit vote. I've employed a good many of them at one time or another in my detective work, and I've looked after their affairs for them.

"But what I want to point out is that we've got to stick together. If we don't, twelve or fifteen rats, all voting together, can upset all our plans. And how would you like it if Simon was president?"

The animals all looked pretty scared, and Mrs. Wogus said: "Freddy! You don't mean there's a chance of that?"

"Not if we stick together," Freddy repeated. "And of course, if he did get elected, we'd all get together and throw him out. But that's revolution, and we don't want a revolution on this farm."

"How about bugs?" asked Hank, the old white horse. "Seems to me if you're going to be so fair to rats, you ought to be fair to bugs, too. Ain't a bug got any rights on this farm?"

"It's kind of funny to hear you standing up for bugs, Hank," said Mrs. Wiggins, "remembering how you pestered the life out of Mr. Bean until he bought some fly poison for the barn, so you could take naps in the afternoon."

"Flies ain't bugs, are they?" said Hank. "They're pests. Still, I dunno; maybe you're right. You got to draw the line somewhere."

"We can't give bugs the vote," said Robert. "Ants and beetles and butterflies and—why, there's millions of 'em. It would take five years to count the votes."

"Yes, and suppose *they* all stuck together and voted alike," said Emma. "Dear me, suppose we had one of those dreadful centipedes for president!"

"That's so," said Freddy. "Bugs are out. Besides, this isn't a bug republic. It's a government of animals, by animals, and for animals. And birds of course," he added with a nod to Charles.

"*And* birds!" said Charles bitterly. "*And* birds!

Why not for birds *and* animals, I should like to know. Why not—"

"No oration, Charles, *please!*" said Freddy. "When we say animals, we mean birds. And anyway, Charles, you're really not a bird. You can't fly."

"Oh, is that so!" shouted the rooster. "And you can, I suppose? Like you did this morning, hey? Can't fly! I suppose you don't remember that time down in the Everglades when I saved all your lives by flying. I suppose—"

"Of course we remember it," said Freddy. "What I mean is that your normal mode of progression—or shall we say locomotion?—is by walking."

"Come again?" said Charles, who, although he used a great many long words in his speeches, seldom knew what they meant, and was wondering if perhaps he oughtn't to get still madder.

"Skip it," said Freddy. "I'm only saying that if you want to go anywhere, you walk. You don't fly. I'm surprised at you, Charles. I've just explained that we all must stand together, and right away you start a row about an unimportant thing like that."

Charles subsided, grumbling in his beak, and Mrs. Wiggins said: "I agree with you about the bugs. But how about Webb?"

"That's right," said Hank. "The Webbs went to Florida. There's stripes for 'em in the flag. But spiders are bugs, ain't they? Or ain't they?"

"They're bugs all right, as far as I know," said Freddy. "But Mr. Webb is a very distinguished bug. And Mrs. Webb is a very charming one. They've certainly got as good a right to vote as anyone on the farm. Now, that *is* a problem."

When Mr. Webb heard his name, he came swinging down his little silk ladder from the roof and landed on Mrs. Wiggins's nose. The cow sniffed and began puckering up her face for a sneeze. "Hey, what in the nation—!" she gasped. "Oh, it's you, Webb. Hang on." And she gave a tremendous sneeze. "Are you there?" she said. "All right, all right; quit clawing me or I'll sneeze again. Get up by my ear."

So Mr. Webb went up close to her ear, and the other animals waited while he talked. "It's all right," said Mrs. Wiggins after a minute. "Webb says he and Mrs. Webb don't care about voting. Says he's a bug and proud of it, but he knows it might cause us trouble, and he's *sure* it would cause him trouble, what with the other bugs being jealous and all. Now, isn't that Webb all over?"

The animals all said it was fine of him and gave him

• • • No oration, Charles, please • • •

a cheer, and Mr. Webb ran up to the tip of Mrs. Wiggins's left horn and jumped up and down, which is a spider's way of showing good feeling.

"Now," said Freddy, "who shall we nominate for president?"

Immediately all the animals began speaking at once. "I nominate Robert!" "Jinx is my choice!" "Freddy! Freddy for president!"

"Our Uncle Wesley always said," quacked Alice, "that he believed I had great executive ability, if I only had a chance to use it. Now, I think—"

"I assure you, ladies and gentlemen," interrupted Charles, "that if this high honor should fall to me—"

"Quiet!" squealed Freddy. "Quiet! Silence! Shut *up!* Don't you see? Don't you see what's going to happen? Jinx is going to vote for Jinx, and Charles for Charles, and Alice for Alice, and so on. We'll all get from one to three or four votes apiece. And the rats will vote in a body for Simon and elect him. We've *got* to agree. Now, I don't say that Alice or Jinx or Charles or anyone here would make a bad president. I don't think there's any one of the old crowd that wouldn't do a good job. But we can't all be elected. We've got to agree on one.

"And I want to say right here that I am not a candidate. For one thing, I don't like to get up early in the morning. And believe me, the president of this farm has got to get up early and stay up late. Now is there anybody else who doesn't want the job?"

"Well, I don't, for one," said Henrietta. "Haven't I got enough to do with twenty-seven children and a husband to manage and pick up after without taking on a whole farm? And Charles doesn't want it either."

"Oh, come, Henrietta," protested the rooster. "If a wide popular demand should be made for my services, could I in all decency refuse? To the clarion call of public duty the private citizen must respond, no matter how great the sacrifice. And who am I to say that—"

"Stuff and nonsense," interrupted Henrietta vigorously. "The wide popular demand is usually for you to shut up, and you can respond to that right now." And she glared at him so ferociously that Charles sighed and, leaning his head against the wall, fell into a reverie.

"I guess there wouldn't be any wide popular demand for me either," said Hank. "There's some days I think I'd like to be a king or a president or something, and lead parades and have the people throw their hats up and cheer when I went to the window. And there's some days I'm glad I'm just Hank, that nobody pays any attention to, and I look out the window and there ain't anybody there looking back at me. And there's other days when I got the rheumatism in my off hind leg and it just kind of hurts me even to smile. If I could just be president on the good days, I dunno's I'd mind. But every day for a year ain't my choice."

Then some of the others said they didn't want to be president either, and Alice withdrew when she found she'd have to make speeches. "Because," she said, "I could never stand up in front of an audience, never."

Finally the choice was narrowed down to Jinx, Robert, Mrs. Wiggins, Eeny, and Ferdinand.

And after some argument Freddy said: "As far as doing a good job goes, I don't think it makes any difference. Any of you would do a good job. But my choice would be Mrs. Wiggins. She's got the presence for it. She's the biggest of us all—and that's very important, for she'll show up well in crowds or group photographs. She's a good mixer. And she's got common sense. Also, she's had some practice in public speaking, in those travel talks she used to give. I think we should all get behind Mrs. Wiggins."

"Well now, Freddy," said Mrs. Wiggins, with a troubled look on her broad face, "I don't agree with you. A cow ain't built for public life, and that's a fact. A cow's place is in the home. Now, I think—"

But Freddy interrupted her quickly. He felt pretty sure that the other animals agreed with him, and he didn't want another argument started, which might split them up again. "Nonsense," he said loudly. "You're our candidate. Go in and win. Mrs. Wiggins for president: that's our platform, and on it we stand. How about it, animals?"

The others, carried away by Freddy's enthusiasm, agreed and shouted down Mrs. Wiggins's objections.

"Well," she said at last, "all right. I'll do my best. If you'll all get behind me, as Freddy says, maybe we'll get somewhere. But," she added with her booming laugh, "if you shove good and hard it'll be better. A cow's awful hard to move."

VIII

A mob of animals of all kinds and sizes jammed the big barn to the doors that evening, and hundreds of late arrivals crowded close up to every crack and door and window, straining their ears to hear every word that was said. Freddy, sitting with his friends in the old phaeton which always served as a platform at these meetings, said to Jinx: "Lots of strange faces here to-night. I don't even know some of these animals. And heavens, there's old Whibley, the owl. He hasn't been out in society in five years. Gosh, there are even a couple of animals that I don't know what they are."

"Coons, I guess," said Jinx. "But they've had their hair combed and their faces washed. Well, Freddy, they're all here. Better get up and give them the works."

So Freddy stood up. Resting one forefoot on the dashboard, which was tastefully draped with the new flag, he raised the other for silence. "My friends," he said, "we have come together here tonight to do something that has never before been done in the history of the world. We have established the First Animal Bank, and now we meet to establish the first animal republic. There is no need to tell you how momentous such an occasion must be. There is no need to remind you of the tremendous results which may follow from our action here tonight, and which will influence the lives of our children and our children's children for generations untold. Nor is there need—"

"If there isn't any need," interrupted Jinx in a stage whisper, "what do you go on yelling about it for? There's no need to talk all night. Get to business."

"Er—no," said Freddy, pulling himself up short. "There is no need for any of these things. So we will proceed to the main business of the evening, which is the nomination of candidates for the office of president. The election will be held in two weeks' time. The meeting is open for nominations."

After the applause died down, there was a moment of silence. Freddy looked down and in the front row saw Simon and his entire family, all staring up at him with their beady black eyes, looking very solemn and innocent. And he was just wondering if they would really have the nerve to nominate one of their number, when a voice in another part of the hall said: "Ladies and gentlemen!" It was John Quincy.

"Ladies and gentlemen," said John Quincy, "what must we look for in the first president of this great new nation? We must look for three things: honesty, brains, and the willingness to do hard work. Now, my experience during my short but happy time in your midst leads me to believe that any of those who may be nominated tonight will possess those three qualities to the full. So far, then, the candidate whom I wish to propose to you has nothing better to offer you. He possesses these qualities, it is true, in the fullest measure. But I am fully aware that there is enough honesty, brains, and willingness to work here in this hall tonight to supply a dozen presidents. A dozen, do I say? Nay, a hundred."

There was wild cheering at this point, but when it had died down, old Whibley, the owl, who had kept his eyes closed during the first part of the speech, opened them, blinked twice, and said in a loud voice: "Talk, talk! I didn't come here to listen to a lot of talk!" But he was shushed down, and John Quincy proceeded.

"But, ladies and gentlemen," he said, "there is another quality which is even more important. It is the ability to avoid making mistakes. It is, in a word, experience. I will be brief. I wish to propose to you as a candidate for the presidency one who has had wide experience, not only of men and cities, but of the way in which a great nation is governed. One who has lived for years, not only in Washington, but actually in the White House grounds. One who has been an intimate of presidents and a close observer of their habits. I nominate Grover."

"Woodpeckers!" said old Whibley disgustedly. "Bug-eaters!" But the cheering drowned his voice. And then Grover was speaking.

"Fellow citizens," he said, "I am a bird of action. I will not bore you with a long speech. My record as president of the First Animal Bank speaks for itself. But there are a few things I should like to tell you. You do not know me well, for I have been with you only a short time. But already I feel one of you. I have cast my lot with you, and I think I can promise that I will do my best for you, whether as a private citizen, as banker, or as president of your—of our, I should say—great country. Now, my friends . . ."

His voice went on, and Freddy turned to Jinx. "Did you see that?" he said. "Simon and his gang cheering for Grover."

"Let 'em," said Jinx darkly. "Their cheering days are pretty near over. What's worrying me is the birds. There are more birds than animals here—did you notice that?—and— But let's wait and see how they take Mrs. Wiggins."

"The test of a good president," Grover was saying, "is: what does he do for the people? And, particularly, what does he do for those who voted for him? Frankly, my friends, this nomination has come as a great surprise to me, and I have not yet had time to consider these matters. But I promise you this: if I am elected—"

"You will be! *Grover forever!*" shouted an enthusiastic blue jay.

"—I will see that those who elected me will have no cause to regret it."

The birds went wild at the conclusion of the speech. They cheered and whistled and clapped their wings, and the noise went on and on until Jinx looked hope-

lessly at Freddy. "This is bad," he shouted. "They'\
elected him already. We mustn't let 'em be so sure.
Can't you do anything?"

Freddy shook his head, but Mrs. Wiggins's broad
face suddenly broke into a smile. "I can," she said.
"Leave it to me." And suddenly she drew in her
breath, and opened her mouth, and let out a tremendous
laugh with the full strength of her lungs. And believe me, when a cow laughs as loud as she can, you sit
up and listen. Lions aren't in it.

The cheering faltered and died down, and in the
silence that followed, Grover said with angry politeness: "Pardon me, but have I—er, said something
funny?"

"Couldn't if he tried," grumbled old Whibley, and
Mrs. Wiggins said: "Dear me, no. I—I just thought
of something." And she laughed again.

"Madam," said Grover between his teeth—at least
that's the way it sounded, though a woodpecker hasn't
any teeth—"Madam, I consider your laughter entirely
out of place. Kindly restrain yourself or leave the
hall."

At this some of the animals looked rather shocked,
for Mrs. Wiggins was a highly respected member of
the community. "Hey, hey," said Jinx. "Aren't we

going to be able to laugh in this new republic if you're president?"

"Laughter," said Grover, "has its place. I should be the last to deny it. But its place is not in government. It is a destructive element."

"Destroys stuffed shirts," said old Whibley in a loud voice. "And a good thing, too."

"Sir!" said Grover icily. "Will you kindly explain that remark?"

"With pleasure," said old Whibley, suddenly waking up and opening his enormous eyes very wide. "I came here as a sober citizen. Didn't come to laugh. Came to hear common sense. Instead, got a lot of windy balderdash. 'Enough to make a cow laugh,' I said to myself. And sure enough, a cow laughed. Well?"

"You're referring perhaps to my speech?" asked the woodpecker.

"Clever of you to guess it," said the owl.

"Sir," shouted John Quincy suddenly, "this is my father you're speaking of."

"Like father, like son," said old Whibley.

"I shall hold you to a strict accounting for those words," said Grover furiously. "Perhaps here in the North such words can be spoken with safety, but not where I come from. A Southern gentleman defends his honor with beak and claws. You shall answer to me, sir."

"Any time, bug-eater. Any time," said old Whibley, and then closed his eyes and apparently went to sleep.

"And you say you're not clever!" said Freddy to Mrs. Wiggins, under cover of the excited buzz of conversation that went round the hall.

"Thought it might stir 'em up," said the cow. "But old Whibley was just a piece of luck. Anyway, it's always safe to laugh and not explain, if the other side seems to be getting the best of an argument. Makes 'em think maybe they've said something foolish and don't know it."

Suddenly Simon was on his feet. "Ladies and gentlemen," he said, folding his forepaws across his chest and looking very saintly indeed, "we are wasting valuable time. And so far only one candidate has been nominated. I gather from certain remarks that have been passed, that there is some objection to this candidate because he is a bird. Though I am an animal myself, this kind of jealousy seems to me petty and foolish. If a bird will make a better president, then, I say, elect a bird. And the birds, I am sure, and all honest animals, will vote for the candidate best fitted for the job, even if he is a bird.

"But, ladies and gentlemen, I suspect that we have not heard all the nominations yet. I have good reason to believe that a certain group of animals have come to this meeting secretly prepared to nominate a candidate, whom they have already elected in their own minds. I say nothing of the secrecy with which they have plotted to grasp the reins of government—"

"Good gracious!" said Mrs. Wiggins to Freddy. "He's turning the birds all against us. Better have Charles begin right away."

For it had been arranged that Charles was to make the speech nominating Mrs. Wiggins. He was a fine orator, with a great gift of language, and yet nothing he said ever meant anything special—which is just what you want in a nominating speech. The trouble was now, though, that everything old Whibley had said about the woodpeckers' speeches would apply even more to Charles's remarks, which were certain to be even windier balderdash than anything heard that evening. The birds would just laugh him down.

"You'd better nominate her," said Freddy to Jinx.

But Charles overheard him, and he jumped up quickly on the dashboard of the phaeton and shouted: "Ladies and gentlemen, friends and fellow vertebrates—" But that was as far as he got, for Jinx pulled him down.

"Hold him, Robert," said Jinx. And as Robert seized the angrily squawking rooster and dragged him down out of sight under the back seat of the phaeton, Jinx addressed the audience.

"Simon is right," he shouted. "He's a thief and a robber, as you all know, but he's right for once. We *have* selected a candidate, and we *are* sure that candidate will be elected. Our red-headed, bug-eating friend has told you that experience is what we want in a president. For once, he's right, too. That *is* what we want. But what kind of experience? This is a republic, but it is also a farm. And the kind of experience we want is not experience in running a big nation, but experience in running a farm.

"And another point: we want someone we know—not a stranger. I nominate Mrs. Wiggins."

The cheering was louder this time than before, partly because animals can make more noise than birds when they set their minds to it, but partly, too, because there wasn't an animal or bird on the farm that didn't like and admire Mrs. Wiggins. You just couldn't help it.

Mrs. Wiggins was too big to get into the phaeton,

but she walked out in front of it, very pleased and flushed, and smiled comfortably at the assembly.

"You're all my friends here," she said. "And among friends we don't need a lot of talk. I don't think I'd make you a specially good president, but if some of you think different, I'll do the best I can." Then she walked back.

Old Whibley opened his eyes wide and nodded approvingly. "Clever speech," he said.

"Clever nothing," said Mrs. Wiggins. "It's the truth."

"That's why it's clever," said the owl.

After that, Freddy called for further nominations, and there was silence for a minute, and then a young rabbit named Marcus got up. He was rather scatter-brained, even for a rabbit, and was always doing things that his people thought quite crazy, but everybody liked him. And he wasn't afraid of anything. Once there had been a fierce bulldog on the Witherspoon place, and he was always chasing the rabbits and scaring them half out of what few wits they had. Marcus's grandfather had been chased by him all one afternoon and had never been the same since. So one night Marcus dressed up in part of an old flour-sack and went over to the Witherspoon place and hid behind a bush,

· · · one night Marcus dressed up · · ·

and when the dog came by he jumped out and said: "Boo!" The dog gave a yelp and ran, and Marcus chased him right out of the county, and he never came back.

So when Marcus got up, nobody laughed, and Freddy smiled at him, and Marcus said: "Now, lookit, Freddy; if anybody asks me, what'll I say is the name of this new republic?"

"Eh?" said Freddy, and then he said: "My goodness, we forgot that, didn't we?"

So then the meeting discussed a name. Jinx wanted to call it Beania, but Freddy didn't like that because he wanted to write a national anthem, and there wasn't any rhyme to Beania, except words like "Armenia" and "neurasthenia," which didn't sound very patriotic.

"Well, how about Animalia?" said Georgie. "You can sing:

We hail ya,
Animalia!
Whenever foes assail ya,
We'll rally round the dear old flag
Of glorious Animalia.

Anyway, there isn't any rhyme to United States, or to America, in *The Star-Spangled Banner*."

But nobody liked that either.

"We can have letters," said Robert. "Like U.S.A. The F.A.R.—First Animal Republic." And after some discussion that was adopted.

"Now, ladies and gentlemen," said Freddy, "if there is no further business before the meeting, we will clear the floor for dancing. But first I want to say that although so far we have only two nominations for president, other nominations can be made at any time before election, which is two weeks from tonight. Or if, on election day, you want to vote for somebody who hasn't been regularly nominated, you can."

Marcus stood up again. "Now—could I vote for myself?" he asked.

"Certainly," said Freddy. "Anybody can vote for anybody he wants to. And now, if there are no more questions . . ."

IX

On a warm spring morning, three days later, Freddy
sat in the bank. He had a frown on his face and a pencil
in his hand. He wasn't doing anything with the frown,
but with the pencil he occasionally jotted something
down on a piece of paper. Then he would sigh and,
putting down the pencil, pick up a palm-leaf fan and
fan himself exhaustedly for a few moments. It was
hot in the bank, which had a door but no windows.
Opposite Freddy's head was a crack between two
boards which extended all along one wall of the bank.
Peeking through it, he could see a group of animals

listening to a campaign speech by Jinx, and the sounds of other campaign speeches drifted through the door. The great presidential campaign was in full swing.

Freddy got up and walked to the door. "Well, here comes Hank, back from the station," he said after a minute, turning toward Grover and John Quincy, who were talking together in low voices in another corner of the bank. "Well, well; the Beans have really gone at last."

"You had better come back and sit down," said Grover. "It doesn't look well for an officer of the bank to be loafing in the doorway during business hours."

Freddy smiled good-naturedly. "It's hot in there," he said. "I don't see how you stand it."

"There's a nice breeze comes through this crack," said John Quincy.

"I'm bigger than you are, and I take a bigger breeze," said Freddy. "It may keep you cool, but I can just barely feel it on the tip of one ear.—Hi, Hank," he shouted, "did you get them on the train all right?"

Hank, pulling an empty buggy behind him, stopped by the wall. "Guess so. Last minute, Mr. Bean remembered he'd forgot his pipe, and wanted to go back for it. But Mrs. Bean said they wouldn't let him smoke a pipe in them fancy foreign hotels, so he bought some cigars. Last I seen of 'em, they was all leanin' out of the car window and wavin' to me. And Mr. Bean with that big cigar. It looks funnier than all get-out on him. Makes me kind of sad, though. Well, guess I'd better get back and get this harness off. Pretty hot for it." And he went on toward the barn.

Freddy went back into the bank.

"Mr. Secretary," said Grover, "I wish to notify you that there is to be a meeting of the board this afternoon at three, to vote for officers."

"Officers!" said Freddy. "The bank has got officers —what do you need to vote for them for?"

"We have to vote for a secretary," said John Quincy.

"But *I'm* secretary," said Freddy. "Say, what is this? Are you trying to get me out?"

"Not at all," said Grover. "But in view of your lack of interest in the affairs of the bank, we feel we should have another secretary—one who will be here during business hours."

Freddy would have been glad enough to get out of the bank, which hadn't been very much fun, particularly since the arrival of Grover. But he wasn't going to be thrown out. And he wasn't going to leave all the things the animals had entrusted the bank with, to say nothing of Mr. Bean's money, in the care of strangers. At least he said to himself that he wasn't. But just how he was going to prevent it he didn't know. He remembered Mrs. Wiggins's advice about laughing, however, and so instead of getting mad he suddenly burst into a loud roar of laughter.

He held his sides and laughed and laughed, and he was pleased to see that the woodpeckers looked first startled, then rather worried.

"What's so funny?" said John Quincy. "See here, Freddy; you know you're not a good secretary for the bank. X will be better and he likes the work. And we're not going to vote you *out*, you know. You'll still be an officer."

Freddy went right on laughing.

"Oh, go ahead and laugh, stupid," said Grover, losing his temper. "Let me tell you, my fine young friend—"

"Father!" interrupted John Quincy warningly. "Perhaps Freddy has a—well, perhaps he knows some reason why we shouldn't vote Xie in his place. Perhaps we should hear his side of it."

"My side?" said Freddy. "Ha ha! You'll hear it soon enough. Go ahead and vote me out and see what happens. Boy, it makes me laugh every time I think of it."

The woodpeckers looked nervously at each other, and Grover said: "Well, well, what we are doing is being done for the good of the bank. I hope for your own sake that you aren't planning anything foolish to get even with us."

"I've got a plan, all right," said Freddy. "Go ahead and have your old board meeting. If I'm not secretary of the bank any more, I don't have to stay here, anyway." And with a final giggle he picked up his pencil and paper and left.

"That laughing is certainly great stuff," he said to himself. "Just the same, I wish I did have a plan. But that will have to wait until after election."

He walked up to the pigpen, went into his comfortable, untidy study, sat down in the old easy chair in which he had composed so many of his immortal verses, and studied the paper over which he had been frowning in the bank.

The paper was well covered with figures in Freddy's careful handwriting. He had used both sides of the sheet and from the appearance he had given the proposition more than a little thought.

This is what he had written on it:

Farmers' Party

Wiggins for President.

Cows	3
Horses	2
Dogs	2
Cats	1
Pigs	1
Mice	4
Ducks	2
Rabbits	176
Skunks	11
Bears	1
Foxes	1
Squirrels	34
Chickens (doubtful)	38
Owls	1?
Chipmunks, mixed animals, incl. field mice	82

After he had studied it awhile he added it up, and it came out 346. Then he added it again, and it came out 365. Freddy wasn't very good at addition.

"Oh, well," he said, "that gives you a rough idea."

So he took another sheet of paper and wrote:

Equality Party
Grover for President

Woodpeckers	7
Rats	21
Robins	18
Sparrows	42
Mixed birds	135
Weasels and assorted small animals (estimated)	65

Then he added these up, and it came out 287 the first time, and 290 the second.

Then he took a third sheet of paper and wrote:

$$\begin{array}{r} 365 \\ -\,290 \\ \hline 74 \end{array}$$

I don't know how he got that 4.

He studied this third paper for a long time, and at last he said to himself: "Well, even if my figures are not quite right, we can't lose. If Charles and all the chickens vote for Grover, still we will have more votes. Pshaw, Wiggins is elected all right. I guess

I'd better get a piece ready for the Centerboro newspaper. Now."

So he blew the dust off his typewriter, and wrote:

WIGGINS WINS

Cow Elected

First Animal Republic President

By an overwhelming majority today the Farmers' Party of the Bean farm's Animal Republic carried their candidate to victory over the suave and courtly Grover, the Equality Party's choice for President. Mrs. Wiggins, after casting her own vote early in the day, remained quietly in her barn, listening to the election returns. When the news of her victory was brought to her, she smiled quietly and said: "I did it all for—"

Here Freddy stopped and shook his head. "No," he said, "that's wrong. That's what they say when they've won a race or something. Let me see, I'll have to think of something good. ' "The people have spoken," she said with quiet dignity. "It only remains for me to—" ' "

Freddy had to stop again at this point, for the door

opened, and John stuck his nose in. "Hi, Freddy. Going to the duel?"

"Duel?" said Freddy. "What duel?"

"Grover and old Whibley. Better come along. It ought to be good."

"Pooh! There won't be any duel," said Freddy. "That was all Grover's talk."

"Sure it was Grover's talk, but he's got to back it up by fighting. He wasn't going to do anything about it, I guess, but a lot of us kidded him about it, and then this morning Jinx was making a speech down by the creek, and he brought it up and said: did we want a president who talked big and made a lot of threats, and then backed down when it came time to fight? And I guess Grover decided he'd lose a lot of votes if he didn't challenge old Whibley to a duel, so he did."

"Gosh!" said Freddy, stuffing his papers into a drawer. "Sure I'm coming. When does it start?"

"I don't know. Old Whibley just laughed when John Quincy brought the challenge, and said: well, as long as he was the challenged party, he had a right to select the time and the weapons, and so he said: 'Beaks and claws at midnight.' John Quincy said: 'That isn't fair. Grover can't see at night.' And old Whibley said: 'That isn't my fault. We fight then or not at all.'

So then John Quincy went back and told his father, and Grover got mad—I guess he thought old Whibley was afraid—and he said he'd go down this noon and force him to fight. So we're all going down to see what happens."

From all directions the animals, their political differences forgotten, were converging toward the woods. The birds, and such animals as could climb, had got seats on branches which had a good view of the entrance to old Whibley's nest, high up in an old gnarled beech. Everybody stared at the entrance, although the owl wasn't visible and Grover had not yet come. Freddy stared until he got a crick in his neck, and then he lay down on his back and looked up that way, which was much easier.

After some time Grover came flying through the trees, followed by John Quincy and X. Freddy thought he looked very determined, but woodpeckers have a sort of determined look anyway, so it was hard to tell. He certainly gave a very determined rap on old Whibley's door with his bill.

"Nothing today," said a voice, and then a young owl came and looked out. She was a niece of old Whibley's named Vera, who kept house for him. "Oh, excuse me," she said. "I thought it was the junk man."

"This is no time for cheap jokes," said Grover. "Tell old Whibley to come out. I have challenged him to a duel and he has got to fight."

"Oh," said Vera, "you've come about the duel. But aren't you early? Uncle was planning to tear you to pieces about midnight. He's gone to have his claws sharpened. Said he didn't want to botch the job—no sense to cause needless suffering. One swift stroke—tear the head right off—that's the kindest thing in the end. That's what Uncle says."

One or two of the listening animals giggled, and Jinx said: "Wow! Is there a doctor in the audience?" But Freddy, because he was lying on his back, saw what none of the others saw—old Whibley sitting on a branch just over Grover's head.

"You tell your uncle to come out," said Grover. "I'm not going to fight him at midnight. I can't see in the dark as he can, and he knows it."

"You won't need to," said Vera. "Uncle never misses."

"If you won't tell him to come out," said Grover angrily, "I'm coming in and pull him out." And he hopped nearer to the entrance.

"Are you indeed?" said Vera, and she reached out one large capable claw and grabbed him by the neck

K·WIESE

· · · Are you indeed? · · ·

and shook him. The feathers flew, and Grover struggled and pecked at her, and John Quincy and X went for her, too. But she was just inside the hole and they couldn't reach her.

"Hey, go easy, Vera," called Jinx, and the other animals began to get worried, for Grover's head was beginning to waggle.

And then old Whibley said: "That'll do, Vera."

Every head in the crowd went up, and there was a murmur of surprise. And old Whibley said: "You've handled this badly, niece. Don't want to kill the creature. Thought I could save myself bother by keeping out of sight. Pshaw!"

He flew down next to Grover, who was saying: "Awk!" and wriggling his neck as if he had a tight collar on. "You see, woodpecker, what chance you'd have in a duel with Vera. Not as strong as me, either. Often given her a good sound spanking when she misbehaved. Eh, niece?"

"That's right, Uncle," said Vera.

"Well. So you want a duel, eh? Suppose you'd be satisfied if I made an apology?"

Grover, who still couldn't speak, nodded.

"H'm," said old Whibley. "What'd I say? Said you were a stuffed shirt. Said you talked a lot of balderdash. True, too. Won't apologize for telling the truth. See here, Grover, you're smart; no coward, either. Why not stop being a stuffed shirt? Stop talking balderdash. Then I could say: Grover *isn't* a stuffed shirt. Grover *doesn't* talk balderdash. Eh? That's the way to settle this. No insult; no duel. Fury! I'm making a speech myself!"

"I *demand* satisfaction," croaked Grover. "I will not be made fun of."

"You'll be made fun of if you're funny," said the owl. "By others, if not by me. Can't fight every animal on the farm. Well, can't talk all day. All right. I apologize."

"You apologize?" said Grover.

"Certainly. You *are* a stuffed shirt, and you *do* talk balderdash, but I apologize for saying so."

"But that's no apology," said John Quincy.

"What do you mean, it's no apology?" said the owl. "Either I apologize or I don't apologize. If I do, it's an apology, isn't it?"

"Yes, but—"

"Let it go, John Quincy," said Grover. "We're not getting anywhere. He doesn't intend to fight. Very well, Whibley, I accept your apology. But kindly keep away from my meetings in the future."

"Certainly shall," said the owl. "Can't stand balder-dash."

Grover, who had started to leave, turned sharply around, but John Quincy said something to him, and he shrugged his wings and the three woodpeckers flew off. Old Whibley closed his eyes.

The crowd, much disappointed that there had been no fight, gradually melted away.

"This business will lose Grover some votes," said Freddy to John. "Old Whibley made sort of a monkey of him."

"I don't know," said the fox doubtfully. "Grover wasn't afraid. It's a good thing to have a president who isn't afraid. How's the election going to go?"

"It'll be a walk-over for Wiggins," said Freddy enthusiastically. "Grover hasn't a chance, not even if the chickens all go over to him. And I don't think they will. Charles is mad at us, but Henrietta controls the chicken vote, and she'll be loyal to the old crowd. And if Charles doesn't vote the way she tells him to, there'll be an empty perch in the warm corner of the chicken-coop after election. I heard her tell him that, so I know."

"That's fine," said John. "I thought you looked worried, and I wondered."

"I'm worried about the bank," said Freddy. "I'd like your advice." And he told the fox about the board meeting. "If I could get in to that meeting," he said, "I could keep them from putting me out. Officers have to be elected by a unanimous vote—in fact, everything the bank does has to be agreed to by all the officers. Listen, John; do you suppose you could give me digging lessons? Maybe I could dig down to the board room."

"You couldn't dig into it in a week even if you had steel claws," said the fox. "You'd need a tunnel nearly three feet across. You're—excuse me, Freddy —you're too fat."

"I know," said Freddy. "My whole family are that way. Fleshy. My father was enormous. A fine figure of a pig, you understand, but—enormous. We like to eat, of course. Pigs do. I expect that's why they call us pigs."

"I remember your father," said John. "When I was little he used to come down to the woods for acorns. We liked him so much. Always a laugh and a joke for everybody. You know, Freddy, it was always my ambition to grow up to be as smooth and sleek and—well, rounded, as he was."

"That's funny," said Freddy. "I've always wanted

to be thin. Always. Sort of slender and willowy. I never saw a pig like that, but I see no reason why one shouldn't be. You know, the first thing I ever wrote had a hero like that. A slim pig. Dear me, what was the title of that?—The Trail of the Lonesome Pig?—no, that was another one. Come down to my study. I'd like to read it to you."

So Freddy forgot all about the board meeting, and he and John spent a happy afternoon reading out loud in the pigpen. And it wasn't until supper time, when John had at last gone home, that Freddy remembered.

Probably he wouldn't have remembered then if John Quincy hadn't come over to tell him the result of the meeting.

"We voted you out and X in as secretary," said the woodpecker. "And then we voted you in again as sixteenth vice-president. So you see you still have your office, but none of the work to do."

"Sixteenth vice-president!" said Freddy. "But there aren't *any* vice-presidents. How can I be six-teenth?"

"Banks always have a lot of vice-presidents," John Quincy explained. "The more they have, the more important the bank is. We just made you sixteenth so it would sound like a more important bank."

"But what do I have to do?" asked the bewildered pig.

"You don't have to do anything. That's just the beauty of it. The vice-presidents don't vote, even, so you don't have to worry about that. The only thing they have to do is if the president is absent, one of them takes his place. It's really an honorary position. Very highly honorary, Father says."

"Too honorary for me," said Freddy. And then he remembered, and instead of saying what he had been going to say, he began to laugh. And John Quincy got mad and left.

But he left without finding out what Freddy really thought about the result of the meeting, and that was just what Freddy wanted him to do. For Freddy didn't have any thoughts about it at all.

X

Wasps as a rule keep to themselves and have little to do socially with their neighbors. But there was one wasp named Jacob who had struck up quite a friendship with Jinx. The cat had been treed by a dog and Jacob had come along and stung the dog on the nose and driven him away. He had done it more as a joke than anything else—wasps have a queer sense of humor —but Jinx had been grateful, and they had had several long talks together. They had found that they both liked to play the same kind of jokes on people, and they could often be seen in a corner of the barnyard snickering over some new mischief they were cooking up.

One day about a week before the election Jacob saw the tip of the cat's tail sticking out of a tangle of bushes down by the lower meadow. He circled around a couple of times, playing with the idea of dropping down and just stinging the tip of the tail gently. But he was really quite considerate for a wasp; he almost never stung his friends, even in fun. So he flew down and crawled into the bushes near Jinx's nose.

"Hello," said the cat. "If you want to see something funny, look out there."

Out in the meadow Freddy was crouching down in the grass, and as Jacob looked, the pig gave a sort of clumsy spring, as if he were pouncing on something. Then he stood up, looked around sheepishly to see if he had been observed, and crouched down again.

"Freddy asked me the other day," said Jinx, "how I got so thin last summer, and I told him I thought it was because I ate so many grasshoppers. That's what Mrs. Bean said, anyway. She advised me not to eat any more of them. So Freddy's gone on a grasshopper diet to see if he can reduce. But of course he can't catch the darn things."

"He'll reduce all right," said Jacob. "Why, he couldn't catch two a day."

The two friends watched for a while, giggling at the pig's ridiculous capers; then Jacob said: "I'm going out and have some fun. Pretend I'm a grasshopper."

"Don't sting him," said Jinx anxiously. "Freddy's a poet, and stings hurt him worse than they do other animals."

"Leave it to me," said Jacob. He went out and swung on a blade of grass a few feet in front of Freddy's nose. Pretty soon the pig saw him. He crouched and crawled closer, but just as he was about to spring, Jacob made a pretty good imitation of a grasshopper jump and landed on Freddy's ear. Freddy made a pass at him, and Jacob jumped to his tail. Freddy whirled, but Jacob was on his ear again. And so it went on, while Jinx rolled on the ground with laughter. And at last Freddy, panting and exhausted, stretched out on the ground. Jacob flew up close to him and said: "Hey, Freddy, don't you want to play any more?"

"Eh?" Freddy gasped. "It's Jacob, isn't it? Darn you, Jacob, is that any way to treat a friend?"

"Why, sure," said the wasp. "You want to reduce, don't you? I was just giving you a little work-out. I bet you've lost five pounds."

"Did you ever think of taking up fancy dancing, Freddy?" asked Jinx, strolling out from the bushes. "I had no idea you were so graceful."

"Oh, it's all very funny to you," said Freddy bitterly. "But you've always been slim and distinguished-looking. You don't know what it is to be fat. I *can* dance well, and I can swim, too, but everybody laughs when I do it. I want to look romantic—like Jacob, here—sort of dark and dangerous-looking. And I *am* romantic—I'm just full of romance inside."

"There must be a lot of it, all right," said Jinx. "No, but really, Freddy, I think you're all wrong about this fat business. Pigs *are* fat. You'd look funny if you weren't. And as far as being romantic goes, my goodness, look at all the things you've done! You've traveled, and you've been a detective, and you've written fine poetry, and what could be more romantic than some of the adventures you've had? I'm sure if anybody said: 'Who is the most romantic animal on this farm?' everybody'd say you were. Wouldn't they, Jacob?"

"Sure would," said Jacob, who was polishing his sting on a bit of moss. "Of course, there's this about fat: some people just sink down into it, and others rise above it. But I'd say you rise above it—all the things

131

you've done. You're a pretty important pig. And you've done it without making anybody mad at you. Why, you've even been fair to us wasps. And most people don't like us much. 'Get out the fly-swatter!'—that's what they say when they see one of us. I'd rather be fat and have people smile when they see me than be romantic-looking and have them try to squash me."

"Well, maybe you're right," said Freddy, brightening a little. "But I've been worried lately. This bank business, and then the election. I don't see how Mrs. Wiggins can lose, and yet Grover seems awfully sure of himself. And there's a lot going on I don't understand."

"Being a bug, the election means nothing to me," said Jacob, "but I don't like birds, and I don't think a bird would be a good president. He'd be too careless. Here's what I mean. You take this Grover. He eats bugs, and I don't hold it against him, for it's his nature so to do. Anyway, he doesn't eat wasps. And that's just what I mean. He doesn't like wasps, and yet if I walk up a tree in front of him, chances are he'll make a grab at me. Why? He'll only get stung. I say birds are careless."

"Well," said Jinx, "I don't eat beetles, but I often make a grab at them. Just for fun."

"You wouldn't if they had stings like this," said Jacob, making a playful pass at the cat, who jumped back with a yowl.

"You see?" said the wasp. "But birds never learn. Look at chickens. There isn't a chicken of my acquaintance who has ever learned that the way not to be run over by an automobile is to get off the road. They jump and squawk and run all over the road and act like fools every time they see one. They never learn. That's why I say that all this talk of Grover's about your needing a president with experience is funny. I don't say he hasn't *had* lots of it, but he hasn't learned anything by it. And so what good is it?"

"What's the point of this lecture?" asked Jinx, who was getting bored.

"The point is that I'm on your side and might be some help. A good sting in the right place might be worth a couple of hundred votes."

"And the right place would be Grover's neck," said Jinx enthusiastically.

But Freddy said: "No. That's decent of you, Jacob, but we can't have violence. You get around a lot, though. I wish you'd keep your eyes and ears open. I'd like to know why Grover is so sure of being elected."

"I can tell you one reason. He's got the chicken vote sewed up."

"Oh, that's just Charles," said Jinx contemptuously. "He's been making a lot of speeches about how birds are nature's aristocrats and the true leaders of the animal world."

"Grover's got Henrietta," said Jacob. "He called on her yesterday and I was sitting on the roof of the henhouse and heard the conversation. He promised her that if he was elected he'd get her a revolving door for the henhouse, and Henrietta promised him all the chicken vote in return. Because she said no matter how many doors they had, the chickens were always trying to go in when others were going out and they were pushing and bumping into one another and it took half her time getting them straightened out."

"But he can't give them that," said Freddy. "It would cost money. That is something for Mr. Bean to decide on."

"Maybe he can't give it to them," said Jacob, "but he's promised, and that's what counts in elections. And I'll tell you another thing, Freddy. Now that he's got you out of the bank and can run it the way he wants to, he's promised that every squirrel and chipmunk and field mouse that votes for him can use the vaults to store his things in free. I heard that speech. 'I pledge you my word,' he said, 'that you will not have to pay one penny for that to which every creature on this farm has an inalienable right—provided he votes for me.' "

"He promised the rabbits a large vegetable garden of their own," said Jinx, "and what he called 'unrestricted right of entry' to Mr. Bean's garden, which I took to mean that they could go in whenever they wanted to. But they didn't fall for it. They know Mr. Bean. Still, I don't know. Some of the rabbits are pretty silly. They might vote for him, at that."

Freddy thought for a minute. Then he said suddenly: "I'm going back and talk to old Whibley. He's got ideas, if you can only get 'em out of him."

"Not me," said Jinx. "I've had enough of his sarcastic cracks."

"He tells you the truth about yourself," said Freddy. "Maybe it'd be a good idea to hear it once in a while."

"Not me either," said Jacob. "My father used to tell me the truth about myself once in a while, and it was usually accompanied with a licking."

So Freddy went back into the woods alone. When he got to the old beech tree, old Whibley was still sitting on the same limb, apparently asleep. Freddy sat down politely and waited.

After a while the owl said: "Well, why don't you say something?"

"I thought you were resting," said Freddy. "I didn't want to disturb you."

"You came here to disturb me, didn't you?" said old Whibley. "So evidently you wanted to. Well then, why put it off?"

"I came to ask you a question."

"Same thing," said the owl.

"Well, anyway," said Freddy, "I know you don't care much about this election, and all you want is to be left alone. But I guess you like Mr. Bean, and we're Mr. Bean's animals, and maybe you'll help me." And he told the owl about his worries.

Old Whibley apparently slept through most of it, and once Freddy was sure he saw his head nod, but when it was finished the owl spread his broad wings and flew down to a branch near the ground and said: "I like you, Freddy. Like you because you do ridiculous things. Can't stand that Grover. He couldn't do a ridiculous thing to save his life. That's why he's ridiculous all the time. Well, see here. These promises of his—revolving door in the henhouse, garden for the rabbits, cat-proof apartments for the rats next the feed-bin— Oh, you hadn't heard about that, eh? Well, how do you suppose he's going to pay for them?"

"He can't," said Freddy. "I suppose they're just promises he can't keep."

"You do, eh? You're forgetting about the bank. Bank's earning two or three dollars a month now, and if he charges twice as much as he does for taking care of things, the animals will pay it. And who's that money belong to, now you're out? Grover."

"Gosh, I didn't think of that," said Freddy. "But that isn't enough money to build all the things he has promised."

"How about Mr. Bean's money the bank has got? Suppose he used that. Mr. Bean comes back. 'Where's my money?' 'Sorry, Mr. Bean,' says Grover. 'We had to use that for necessary improvements.' What's Mr. Bean going to do? Go to law with a woodpecker? He'd rather lose his money than look as silly as that."

"Yes, but—" Freddy began.

"Don't *talk*," said old Whibley severely. "Let me do the talking. That's why you're here, isn't it?"

He didn't say anything for a while—just sat there with his eyes closed, and this time Freddy was certain he heard him snore. But after a while he opened his eyes and said: "Who dug those new vaults for you?"

"John," said Freddy.

"A fox," said the owl. "H'm. Ten to one there's another entrance to them, then. Never knew a fox to dig a hole with only one way out. 'Tisn't natural for them. Now listen to me . . ."

So Freddy listened for quite a while, and then he went off to find John.

He found him with some of the other animals painting signs to be carried in the big Wiggins parade that evening, and drew him aside.

"I didn't tell you, Freddy," said the fox, when Freddy asked him point-blank if there was another entrance to the vaults, "because I knew I oughtn't to do it. But a fox can't any more go into a hole that hasn't two ways out than he can fly. He just can't. Well, there's a hole behind the stone wall back of the bank, and it goes straight down to the board room. It's covered up in the board room so nobody will notice it. Now I do hope you aren't going to say anything about it to Grover. I guess he'd be pretty sore, and—"

"You keep as quiet about it as I do," said Freddy, "and there'll be no trouble. See you later."

Peter, the bear, was poking about among the wild raspberry bushes at the edge of the woods when Freddy found him.

"Well, salt-and-pepper me if it isn't Freddy!" said Peter. "Well, how are you, Freddy? That's a foolish question, though. I can see you're fine. Fat as butter."

"Thanks for nothing," said Freddy. "I've heard about enough of that fat talk today."

"Why, what's the matter with that? Finest compliment you can pay a bear. But we have to be fat because we sleep all winter. Well, maybe you don't like it, but it's very becoming to you. I was just looking over these raspberries. Doing a little pruning and so on. Going to have a nice crop next fall. You must come up and have a dish of them with me some day when they're ripe."

"Like to," said Freddy. "I expect raspberries aren't very fattening. Say, Peter, I've got a little digging job I wonder if you'd do for me."

Peter said there was nothing he'd like better, so Freddy took him down to the stone wall behind the bank, and sure enough, there was a hole just large enough for a fox.

"Want it enlarged to fit you, eh?" said Peter. "Let's see, you take about a 44? Leave it to me. It'll fit you like a glove." And he began digging.

"Not too tight," said Freddy anxiously. "I don't want to get stuck."

Peter's head was already out of sight, and the stones and dirt were flying all around Freddy. Freddy turned his back, hunched his shoulders, and kept a sharp lookout for the woodpeckers. But he was perfectly safe; politics were absorbing the attention of every bird and animal on the farm.

Freddy turned his attention back to the digging.

Peter went deeper and deeper into the hole and finally disappeared, but dirt continued to fly out. It looked like a small volcano in eruption. After a while it stopped, and there was a scrabbling underground and Peter came out, head first. "There you are," he said. "All ready for a fitting. Try it on, and if it's a little too snug under the arms, we'll alter it free of charge."

So Freddy went down. He didn't like crawling down holes much, so he went down backwards. "If I decide to come out in a hurry," he said to himself, "it will be pleasanter to come out head first." But the hole wasn't bad. It was almost straight down, but it was short, and when he got into the board room there was enough light from above so that he could look around. Not that there was much to see. The roof was a big flat rock, and the walls were dirt, with a small hole in one of them which was the tunnel up to

· · · · Want it enlarged to fit you, eh? · · · ·

the bank. Freddy shoved a couple of loose stones into the tunnel and packed dirt around them. "Guess the room's woodpecker-proof now," he said with a grin. Then he went up and thanked Peter, and after sneaking along behind the stone wall until he was some distance from the hole, came out and trotted down to the bank.

Just as he got there, the twelve o'clock whistle blew in Centerboro, and, punctual to the second, Grover and John Quincy came out of the door.

"Good noon, gentlemen," said Freddy politely. "Off to lunch?"

"Yes," said John Quincy. "Where are you lunching, Father?"

"I thought of trying that oak down beyond the barn," said Grover. "The beetles are very good there."

"I have to make one or two calls before lunch," said John Quincy. "Meet you at the oak in half an hour. So long, Freddy."

"Just a minute," said the pig. "I wanted to ask you when the next board meeting is to be held."

"What difference does it make to you?" said Grover. "You can't vote at it."

"I do if the president isn't there and I have to take his place."

"The president will be there, don't worry," said John Quincy. "The meeting's this afternoon at three, though, if you want to know."

"Well, there's another thing," said Freddy. "I've decided I'd like to be president of the bank."

"Have you indeed?" asked Grover sarcastically, and John Quincy said: "Freddy, are you crazy? We just voted you out—do you think we'd vote you in again?"

"Well," said Freddy humbly, "I just thought maybe you were tired of the job. And I'd like it. And I do think the board should vote on it."

The woodpeckers started to argue, but Freddy was determined, and he argued back at them, and finally Grover said impatiently: "Well, I'm in a hurry. I can't stand here all day. All right, Freddy, all right. The meeting this afternoon will vote on whether or not you are to be president of the bank. And I hope you'll like its decision," he added dryly.

"I will abide by its decision," said Freddy.

"Yes," said Grover. "So will we, you may be sure." And with a short laugh he flew away.

Freddy laughed too, after they had gone, and then he hurried back to the board room to wait for three o'clock. He slept awhile, and he spent an hour or so composing a national anthem for the F.A.R., and at last, at two minutes of three, he heard a faint scraping and rustling in the blocked-up passageway that led to the bank, and he knew that the woodpeckers were coming to the meeting. He waited until it was exactly three o'clock. On the other side of the stones and dirt with which he had blocked the tunnel he could hear Grover and John Quincy talking together in low, excited tones. And then he said in a loud voice:

"In the absence of the president of the First Animal Bank of Centerboro, I, Freddy, sixteenth vice-president, declare the board meeting open."

"Hey, Freddy, what's all this? How'd you get in there? Let us in!" shouted the woodpeckers, but Freddy paid no attention and went quickly on.

"The first business before the meeting is the election of Freddy as president. I move that Grover and John Quincy and X be fired from their positions in the bank, and that Freddy be appointed president. I second the motion. Motion made and seconded. All in favor say 'aye.' Aye. All opposed say 'no.' Motion carried."

He had gabbled the words as fast as he could get them out, for he could hear the woodpeckers hammering and digging away with their strong beaks, and he was afraid they would get in before he had finished.

But now he stopped and shouted: "What's all that noise out there?"

The dirt in the passageway crumbled and a beak came through.

"Hey, Freddy!" it called. "Stop the meeting! We're here."

"Well, upon my soul!" said Freddy in a tone of great surprise, as John Quincy's head came poking through the dirt. "Why, I thought you'd been detained somehow, and of course the meeting had to go on. Here, let me help you." And he began digging at the stones.

"This is a very strange business," said Grover, when the two woodpeckers, panting and covered with dirt, stood in the board room. "One of your tricks, eh, my friend? Well, now since we are here, the meeting can begin."

"The meeting's over," said Freddy. "It was announced by you for three o'clock, and as you weren't here at three, I acted as president. Those are the rules, and you can't deny it. And as a matter of fact, since you are no longer officers of this bank, you have no business here, and I must ask you to leave."

"What!" said John Quincy. "It's a trick! It's cheating, Freddy."

"Sure it's a trick," said the pig. "Just as it was a

trick by which you got me out of the bank. Now we're even, and I'm president. And you aren't even seventy-fifth vice-presidents, either. Listen, boys. Let me give you a word of advice. When you play a mean trick on anybody, you want to go the whole way. You want to be as mean as you can. You should have thrown me out of the bank entirely, not left me in. That was your mistake. And now I think you'd better go. People not connected with the bank are not allowed in the vaults."

The woodpeckers looked at him in silence. He thought for a minute that Grover was going to fly at him. But then they turned and went back into the tunnel. Just as he left the board room, Grover turned.

"You'll hear more of this," he said darkly.

"Ah," said Freddy, "so will you. It's too good a story to keep. I expect all our friends will have a good laugh over it."

Grover gave the nearest thing to a growl that a woodpecker can give—it is really a rather faint squeak —and disappeared.

XI

The big Wiggins parade that night was one of the finest things of its kind ever seen in Centerboro—or anywhere else, for that matter. Promptly at seven o'clock it formed and marched out of the barnyard. First came Jinx, walking on his hind legs, with a red, white, and blue scarf over his shoulder, and carrying a drum major's stick, which he twirled expertly, and sometimes even threw up in the air and caught as it came down. At least he tried to catch it, but he didn't always succeed, so that after a while whenever he threw it up the whole parade would break and run for cover, and Mrs. Wiggins had to ask him to stop.

Behind Jinx came Freddy, carrying the red, white, and blue flag of the F.A.R. He had dressed up in one of the many costumes which he used as disguises in his detective work—the white robe of an Arab sheik, which like most of his disguises was much too long for him, so that he kept tripping over it. And once he walked right up inside the robe, and the parade had to be held up to get him untangled. But when he was not tripping, he looked very distinguished.

Behind Freddy came the band—a group of mixed animals who blew on grass stems and rattled tin cans and made other semi-musical noises. Of course, none of the animals could really play anything, but it made a good lot of noise and sounded quite martial. Sometimes they sang, and that was really quite nice. Freddy had written a campaign song, the chorus of which went:

Then vote for Wiggins, everyone,
    Your friend both true and tried;
In peace and war, in storm and calm,
    Let Wiggins be your guide.

The animals sang this, and they sang their marching song, which Freddy had written to the music of *The Battle Hymn of the Republic:*

There's a muttering of marching feet upon
the windless air;
Far across the peaceful hills of Bean the dis-
tant torches flare;
For the animals are coming, you can hear the
trumpets blare
And the drums beat victory.

Hail, all hail to Mrs. Wiggins;
Hail, all hail to Mrs. Wiggins;
Hip, hurray for Mrs. Wiggins,
For our next Pres-i-dent!

In our hundreds and our thousands we are
marching through the night
Underneath the tossing banners, in the
torches' smoky light,
We sing our song of triumph, and we shout
with all our might
For Wiggins—and victory!

When the Farmers' Party marches let all
other parties cower;
We will shatter and defeat them with our
overwhelming power;

We will scatter them like chickens in a sud-
          den thundershower
   As we march to victory!

Hail, all hail to Mrs. Wiggins!
Hail, all hail to Mrs. Wiggins!
Hip, hurray for Mrs. Wiggins,
       For our next Pres-i-dent!

When they sang it all together, it was truly inspir-
ing.

After the band came the carriage of state, which
was the old phaeton that the animals had brought back
from Florida, drawn by Mrs. Wiggins's sisters, Mrs.
Wurzburger and Mrs. Wogus. And in it was Mrs.
Wiggins. Freddy had insisted that there must be a carriage of state, and that she must ride in it. The cow
had protested that she'd never be able to get into the
thing, but Freddy was firm. "We'll get you into that
back seat," he said, "if every animal on the farm has
to help push you in." And it did take a good deal of
pushing. But I must say she looked very impressive sitting there among the banners and the crepe-paper dec-
orations, bowing graciously to the cheering crowds
along the line of march.

Bertram added a good deal to the impressiveness of the carriage. He sat on the front seat, and every few seconds he would shout: "Vote for Wiggins and Prosperity!" at the top of his lungs. Or, rather, at the top of Ronald's lungs, for the rooster was sitting in the little control room inside Bertram. The animals had wanted to have Bertram march in the parade, but Ronald had tried him out, and he said it wouldn't be safe. "Ever since his fall," Ronald said, "Bertram has acted queer. His machinery doesn't work properly. I know what it is, all right. It's when you start to have him do something with his right arm. I could march him, I guess, without any trouble, but I might forget and do something with that right arm, and goodness knows what he might do."

The carriage of state was followed by a detachment of rabbits in paper hats, led by Georgie, and then Hank, all trimmed up with crepe paper and Mrs. Bean's feather duster on his head for a plume. The mice rode on his back. Then came the skunks and the squirrels and some of the other smaller animals, doing fancy marching. They had been drilling hard for a couple of weeks, and their evolutions were received with hearty applause, even from their political opponents. And last came Peter, the bear, at the head of a contingent of woods animals—foxes and raccoons and a porcupine or two.

Many of the animals carried signs, on which were printed such slogans as: "Vote for Wiggins, the People's Friend" or "Win with Wiggins" or "Every Vote for Wiggins is a Vote for Prosperity and Mr. Bean." Alice and Emma had wanted to carry a sign reading: "Hail to Wiggins, Centerboro's Fairest Daughter!" but Freddy had pointed out that that sounded more like a beauty contest than an election, and so they had left the last part off. They probably wouldn't have, for, shy and retiring as they were, they were pretty stubborn, but neither of them could spell "daughter," so they abandoned the idea.

Now, of course it was night when the parade started, and the thing that made it the success that it unquestionably was, was the illumination. With the help of Jacob, Freddy had got together nearly a thousand fireflies, and they kept swooping and flitting over the heads and through the ranks of the marchers and lighting in rows on the phaeton. The head firefly had rather a genius for organization, and he had arranged it so that different parts of the parade were lit up at different times. And sometimes two or three hundred fireflies would light on Jinx or Freddy or on one of the signs, and then twinkle their lights rapidly, which gave a very striking and pleasing effect.

The parade went three times round the barnyard, then up the road, along the rail fence to the woods, down the creek, and back by the upper pasture and the chicken-house, coming out into the road below the First Animal Bank. Mrs. Wiggins made a short speech every time the parade stopped at one of the important points en route. She was not a very eloquent speech-maker, like Charles, or a very political one, like the woodpeckers, but she was earnest, and what she said always meant something, even if it didn't sound beau-tiful. When the parade stopped at the henhouse, Hen-rietta and all her family came out to listen—more out of politeness than anything else, for they didn't intend to vote for her. Charles was there, too, but he kept in the background, for he had had a fight with Henrietta about the parade. He had wanted very much to march in it, but Henrietta had said no, if he wasn't going to vote for Mrs. Wiggins he ought not to parade for her.

"But we're old friends and traveling companions, Mrs. Wiggins and I," Charles protested. "I'm afraid she'll feel hurt."

"That's as may be," said Henrietta. "Anyway, you're not going. And I guess nobody'll notice you aren't there."

So Charles complained a little, and then stayed home.

"Friends and chickens," said Mrs. Wiggins, "for I know you're my friends, whether you vote for me or not—you have been promised by Grover, my worthy opponent, that if he is elected he will get you a revolving door for the chicken-house."

"Hurrah for Grover!" shouted someone in the crowd.

"Quite right," said Mrs. Wiggins. "Hurrah for Grover as much as you want to. But he's made you a promise he can't keep."

"He can too," shouted Henrietta. "He's president of the bank, and he makes lots of money."

"I guess, Henrietta," said Mrs. Wiggins with her broad smile, "you're a little behind the times. Freddy is president of the bank now. Grover has nothing more to do with it."

"Well, if that's true—" Henrietta began, but a loud voice from the roof of the henhouse interrupted her.

"Ladies and gentlemen—"

Everybody looked up, and there was Grover. He

had been quietly following the parade in the darkness, waiting for a chance to break in on the speechmaking.

"It *is* true, ladies and gentlemen," he shouted. "I am no longer president of your bank. But why? Ah, let me tell you why. That pig there"—he pointed a claw at Freddy—"has voted me out. By a mean, cowardly, and dishonest trick he has—"

"Here, here," said Henrietta severely. "No calling names, woodpecker. Freddy is a friend of mine, even if we are on opposite sides in this election. And I have never known him to do anything either mean or dishonest or cowardly, to say nothing of doing them all together. Freddy, take off that nightgown and come up here and tell us the truth about this business."

So Freddy came forward and told the whole story—how by calling meetings in a board room that he couldn't get into, the woodpeckers had voted him out of his office in the bank, and then how by using the same trick, and with the help of Peter, he had voted them out and himself in.

The chickens burst into shrieks of cackling laughter when he had finished, and Henrietta said: "Well, this alters matters. I did want that revolving door, but I haven't been satisfied any of the time that we were doing the right thing in voting for a stranger. Mrs. Wiggins, I'm happy to tell you that you will get all our votes."

"Then I can join the parade?" said Charles eagerly.

"We'll all join the parade," said Henrietta. "Lead on, Jinx. Fall in, girls." And two by two the chickens, giggling and nudging one another, fell into line behind the carriage of state.

All this time Grover had been trying to break in and say something, but each time he had been shushed and shouted down. Now as the parade started on he gave three loud squawks, and at the signal dozens of birds came swirling and swooping above the procession and began gobbling up the fireflies. In two minutes the only fireflies left who had not ducked for cover or been eaten were half a dozen that had taken refuge on Mrs. Wiggins's broad nose, where none of the birds dared to peck at them.

"Well," said Mrs. Wiggins, looking around, "I guess that ends this procession. Rather smart of Grover, I must say."

"It was a good procession while it lasted," said Jinx. "And we've got the chicken vote back. Come on, animals. Dismissed. Home to bed, everybody."

"Hey, wait a minute," said Mrs. Wiggins. "You can't leave me here in this thing."

· · · Now I am stuck · · ·

Now, it is hard enough to get a cow into a carriage, but it is three times as hard to get her out of one. Mrs. Wurzburger and Mrs. Wogus pulled the phaeton down past the bank and into the road where it was level and Mrs. Wiggins tried to get out. First she got her horns tangled in the canopy of the phaeton, and then in trying to get loose she got wedged tightly into the space between the back seat and the back of the front seat.

"Now I *am* stuck," she said hopelessly. "No use pushing, Freddy. I just get stuck tighter."

"If we push hard enough, something's got to give," said Freddy. "Come on, now, Hank, Peter—one, two, *three*."

The animals gave a shove, the phaeton gave a creak and a rattle, Mrs. Wiggins gave a groan, and then the onlookers gave a cheer. For Mrs. Wiggins shot out of the phaeton onto the road, and the animals who had been shoving shot out on top of her. And for a minute they all lay there in a heap, which shook and trembled oddly. But that was Mrs. Wiggins laughing underneath.

"More like a football game than a presidential election," she said, when they had all got up and were brushing themselves off. "Well, well—no bones broken. But after this I do my electioneering on the hoof. No more state carriages for me. I'm not built for them, and that's a fact."

On the way home Henrietta drew Freddy aside.

"If you want Mrs. Wiggins to win this election, you've got to get busy, my friend," she said.

"Pooh," said the pig. "With the chickens on our side, we'll win in a walk."

"Oh, yes?" said Henrietta. "How about all these birds that have been coming and building nests in Mr. Bean's trees? There's hundreds of new ones. And they live here; they can all vote."

"What?" said Freddy. "You mean that Grover—?"

"I mean that Grover and John Quincy and X have been showing some sense," said the hen sharply. "While you've been going around and making speeches to get votes that you're going to get anyway, the woodpeckers have been getting birds in here from all over the country. I wouldn't be at all surprised if they had got enough already to swing the election. They live here, don't they? How can you prevent them voting? No more than you can prevent them from going back, after election, to where they came from. You'd better get busy, Freddy."

XII

A meeting of the leaders of the Farmers' Party was held in the cow-barn next morning to talk over what could be done to combat this new danger. Ferdinand, the crow, who, although a bird, was still faithful to Mrs. Wiggins, reported that on a scouting trip through the woods and the upper part of the farm he had seen more than fifty new nests. "And with each nest containing at least two voters," he said, "you can see where that leaves us."

Freddy had his pencil out and was figuring. "Even with the chickens on our side," he said after a few minutes of intense concentration, "Grover can win by about seventy-five votes."

"This is a fine business!" said Jinx. "Here we are, a dozen or so of us, who have been with Mr. Bean and done everything of importance that has been done on this farm for years. And we're turning over the whole farm to be run by a lot of strange birds who haven't lived here any time at all."

"Well," said Mrs. Wiggins, "I guess it's our own fault. We ought to have made a rule that nobody could vote who hadn't lived here a certain length of time. But as long as we didn't, and as long as we think it's all right for Grover to bring in a lot of outside voters, I don't see why we can't do the same thing."

"More birds?" asked Jinx doubtfully.

"I don't care what they are, as long as we're sure they'll vote our way. But certainly we've got more friends in this countryside than a stranger like Grover. Naturally, we can only bring in small animals, since they'll have to live here for a while. We couldn't feed a hundred cows—not if they've got appetites like mine. But there's room in the different barns and sheds around the place for a thousand small animals, and there are hundreds of unoccupied trees up in the woods. Free board and lodging for the rest of the summer in pleasant surroundings—where's the animal that wouldn't jump at the chance?"

"Gosh!" said Jinx enthusiastically. "That's a swell idea. What a president you'll make! Come on, boys. Scatter. Get busy. I'm going down the valley to the flats, where all those field mice live. They owe me a favor or two. I caught their head man one night two years ago—I just caught him for fun; I haven't eaten a mouse since I was a kitten, but they didn't know that. So they all came out and begged me to let him go, and one of his sons even volunteered to be eaten in his place. He was much fatter and tenderer and of course was a good trade, just considered as something on the bill of fare. I was really quite touched. I made them a little speech, and let him go, and they said if there was ever anything they could do for me— Well, now they can.

"Only there's one thing. We'll have to provide transportation. It's three miles to the flats."

"I'll take the buggy down," said Hank.

"That's fine," said Jinx. "Then I can get a ride down myself."

So the animals all started out to hunt for voters, but Freddy went back to his study to prepare the ballots for the election, which was now only three days away. The plan was to give each animal two pieces of paper when he came to the polls, one with a G on it for Grover, and one with a W for Wiggins. Then he would drop the initial that stood for his candidate into the ballot-box.

Freddy tore some paper into squares and started to work, but he had done only about twenty W's when, glancing out of the window, he saw a man strolling through the barnyard. He was a small plump man who walked with short, quick steps and he had a face a little like a pig's, which made Freddy mistrust him at once. For he said to himself: "When a pig has a face like a pig's, it's only natural. But when a man has a face like a pig's, there's something wrong somewhere."

So he went out and ran after the man, who was walking past the house and pretending that he wasn't trying to peek in the windows.

"Excuse me," said Freddy, "is there anything I can do for you?"

"Deary me!" said the man, turning around with a very bright smile. "What a nice little piggy! And you can talk, piggy. Isn't that lovely!"

"My name is Freddy," said the pig. "And if there is anything I can do for you, please let me know. If not, I'm afraid—"

"You'll go get all the other little piggies," interrupted the man, smiling even more brightly, "and drive me off the place. Is that it? And quite right, too. You must defend your master's property, like a brave little piggy."

"Please stop calling me a piggy," said Freddy crossly. "I told you my name."

"You did indeed," said the man. "And a very pretty name it is. Well, well, I mustn't be thrown off the place by a piggy, so I had better tell you what I am doing here, hadn't I? Well, I am interested in banks. Yes, I think I may say I am very much interested in banks. And I heard there was an animal bank on this farm, so I just dropped in to get a look at it. Deary me! A bank for animals! What won't they have next!"

"The bank is down the road a little way, on the left," said Freddy.

The man thanked him, but he didn't go. Instead he turned and looked at the house. "And so this is the famous Bean farm," he said. "You said the family were away?"

"I didn't say so," said Freddy, "but they are. And now, if you'll excuse me, I have some business to attend to. Good morning."

"Business!" said the little man. "Deary me, what a

farm this is, to be sure! A piggy with business to attend to!" And he laughed heartily.

But Freddy didn't wait any longer. He didn't like the man, and he didn't trust him. Of course the Bean animals were known all over the country, and their exploits had been written up in newspapers and magazines, and people often came to see them and take their pictures and exclaim over them and generally act, as Jinx said, "as if we were Niagara Falls or something." Such people were a nuisance, but usually they weren't anything worse than rather silly. Freddy felt about this man, however, that there was something wrong about him, and so instead of going to work when he got back into his study, he watched through the window.

The man walked all around the house, looking at it carefully, and smiling all the time. He peeked in the windows and even tried the door. And then he went off with his little quick steps toward the bank. "Oh, dear!" said Freddy, and he hurried out and down to the bank the back way, and when the man got there he was sitting behind the counter.

"Deary me!" said the man, as he came in the door. "*Another* piggy! A banker piggy. Will wonders never cease?"

"I'm the same piggy," said Freddy. "That is, I'm Freddy. And stop calling me piggy, will you?"

"Certainly, my little piggy-wig, certainly," said the man. "No offense, now. I just wanted to have a look at your charming bank. You have a good deal of money on deposit, I suppose? Actual cash, that is?"

"We don't give out information to strangers," said Freddy.

"Quite right," said the man. "Very sound practice. And your safe-deposit vaults, now—they're just under the floor?"

Freddy didn't say anything.

"Deary me, I'm afraid you don't like me, piggy-wig," said the man. "And I'm very fond of piggies—yes, I am."

"With plenty of gravy, I suppose," said Freddy sarcastically.

"Well, that's one way of looking at it," said the other. "That's certainly one way of looking at it." And he gave Freddy one of his too bright smiles, and said good morning, and left.

"If he comes around here again," said Freddy to the squirrel on guard at the vault entrance, "let me know right away. The bank is going to be closed until after election, but I want you or one of your brothers to be on guard all the time."

"Yes, sir," said the squirrel respectfully, and Freddy watched the man through the window until he was out of sight round a bend in the road; then he went back to the study. And there was John.

"News for you, Freddy," said the fox. "There's another candidate for the presidency."

"What!" said Freddy. "Do you realize how many of these things I've had to make out? Three hundred W's and three hundred G's, and now even that won't be enough. Now I've got to make out a whole new set?"

"Guess you have," said John. "Marcus is going to run."

"Marcus!" Freddy exclaimed. "That rabbit? Why, nobody'd vote for him. Is it a joke or something?"

"I don't know what it is," said John, "but there's something funny about it. Marcus just announced it at a meeting Grover was speaking to in the woodshed. Grover let him talk, and even got up and congratulated him when he said he wanted to run for president. Grover said he showed fine public spirit, and he welcomed him as a worthy opponent, or something like that. And then yesterday I saw Simon talking to Marcus down by the duck pond. There's some trick in it, and Grover and Simon are both in it."

"Probably a trick on me," said Freddy. "That's three hundred M's I'll have to get ready now. Nobody'll vote for a rabbit, but I suppose I'll have to give them a chance, and that means an M ticket for everybody.

"It's a queer thing, though," he said after a minute. "I agree with you, John, there's some plot of Simon's and Grover's behind it. But I can't for the life of me figure out how they will benefit by it."

They talked for a while about the political situation, and then John's quick ears caught the sound of a horse's hoofs coming up the hill at a trot. They ran out as the hoofbeats broke into a gallop and came nearer and nearer until in through the gate dashed Hank, drawing behind him a buggy crammed to the dashboard with field mice, who were singing and shouting and yelling: "Faster! Faster!" at the top of their lungs.

"What's got into Hank?" said Freddy. "He hasn't run like that in ten years."

The buggy circled the barnyard once and then stopped, and the mice piled out. There were about a hundred of them, and a wild crew they were. "Hurray for the F.A.R.!" they shouted. "When do we eat? Where's the place we're to live in?"

• • • the sound of a horse's hoofs • • •

"Where's Jinx?" Freddy asked Hank.

"They pushed him out down the road about a mile," Hank panted. "You'd ha' laughed yourself sick, Freddy. Bunch of mice gangin' up on a cat. They yelled to me to run away from him and let him walk home. Then Jinx got mad, and I was afraid he might hurt some of 'em, so I did run. Well, I dunno—maybe it seemed kinda funny to me, too. Anyway, I ran. —Here's Jinx now."

The cat, very dusty and out of breath, loped in the gate. Then he stopped and stared at the field mice, his whiskers twitching angrily, and the mice quieted down at once, although they kept giggling and nudging one another.

"Smart, hey?" he said. "Well, you're too smart for us. Go on home, the lot of you. We don't want you. Maybe a three-mile walk will cool you off a little."

"Hey, wait a minute," put in Freddy. "We need these mice, Jinx. You can't send 'em back after you went all the way down to get 'em."

"It was just a joke," said one of the mice. "But if the cat can't take it, why, sure, we'll go home. He was pushing us around in the buggy and having a swell time, and then when we pushed back, he don't like it."

"How about it, Jinx?" said Hank. "You really want

170

to send 'em back and lose all these good votes?"

"Well," said Jinx, "I don't like mice playing jokes on a cat. It—it isn't dignified. And you'd better not try it again," he said, glaring fiercely at the mice, "or I may forget myself.

"All right, Freddy," he added, turning away. "You show 'em their quarters. I want nothing more to do with them." And he stalked off.

All that afternoon the new settlers came marching into the barnyard. Georgie and Robert collected fifty rabbits from neighboring farms and persuaded them, with a promise of free lettuce and protection from hawks and weasels, to set up housekeeping in the lower meadow. Ferdinand flew twenty miles north and interviewed a cousin of his who was chief of a large band of robber crows that lived in the high woods and flew out daily to plunder the neighboring farms. The chief, whose name was Lester, held out for a high price, but finally agreed, for ten sacks of corn, to bring the band down and settle in Mr. Bean's woods for a week, until after election. By night there were several hundred new citizens of the F.A.R., all of whom could be counted on to vote the straight Wiggins ticket. Mrs. Wiggins's election, Freddy felt, was assured.

XIII

Although feeling had run pretty high on both sides, it was on the whole a good-natured crowd that gathered in the barnyard on election day. The animals formed in a long line to enter the voting-place. Inside were Freddy, Jinx, and Mrs. Wiggins, representing the Farmers' Party, and the three woodpeckers, representing the Equality Party. Marcus, who called himself the Opportunity Party, for no very good reason, since he hadn't thought up any opportunity to offer, represented himself, and had Simon with him. The rabbit was rather subdued and nervous, but old Simon seemed in the best of spirits and kept grinning wickedly to himself.

The first animal to vote was one of the field mice, who had sat up all night in order to be at the head of the line.

"Name?" asked John Quincy.

"Winthrop," said the mouse.

"Address?"

"Hayloft. Bean Farm."

"Anybody here to answer for this animal?" asked John Quincy.

"I can," said Freddy. "He lives here."

"Very well," said John Quincy, and handed the mouse three pieces of paper, one with a G, one with a W, and one with an M. "Go into the box stall," John Quincy instructed him, "and drop the paper with the initial of the candidate you want to vote for into the feed-box in the corner. Then bring the other two papers out with you and drop them in this barrel."

So the mouse went into the stall, and the next voter, an oriole named W. F. Jessup, stepped forward. He gave his address as Twin Maples, Upper Pasture, Bean Farm, and when X had vouched for him, he followed the mouse.

And so the voting went on. By noon eight hundred votes had been cast, and as they were beginning to run out of ballots, fresh sets of three had to be made up out of those discarded in the barrel. By two o'clock the last vote had been cast. It was the eleven hundred and sixty-first.

"Now," said Grover, "we'll count 'em."

They rolled the barrel of discarded ballots outside, so that they couldn't get mixed up with the others, and brought in the feed-box. The ballots were dumped out on the floor, and the animals began busily sorting them into piles.

After ten minutes or so, when Freddy had thirty-four W's and twenty-two G's in front of him, he looked up. "My goodness," he said, "I just thought—" Then he stopped. "Good gracious!" he said to himself, and looked. Mrs. Wiggins and Jinx both had two piles in front of them, but the woodpeckers and Marcus and Simon each had three piles, all about equal in size.

Freddy went over and whispered to Jinx and Mrs. Wiggins, then he said: "Wait a minute."

The others all looked up, and Simon snickered.

"I just want to see how we're getting on," said Freddy. "Grover, how many have you got now? We'll want to send out a preliminary bulletin. All the voters are waiting out there in the barnyard."

"I have twelve for Wiggins, twenty-six for Marcus, and nineteen for myself," said Grover.

"You actually believe that twenty-six animals voted for Marcus?" asked Freddy.

"There are twenty-six M's," said the woodpecker. "I gather from that that twenty-six animals voted for him."

"But those aren't M's," said Jinx, looking over Grover's shoulder. "They're W's."

"Look like M's to me," said Grover. "Come, let's get on with the count."

"No," said Mrs. Wiggins firmly. "We'll get this decided right now. I see what your plan was, Grover, in persuading Marcus here to run. You could take my W votes and read them upside down, and of course they are M's. Then a lot of the votes that ought to be counted for me would be counted for Marcus, and you'd have more votes than I would. Actually, probably the only vote cast for Marcus was the one he cast himself."

"I voted for him, for one," said Simon with his oily smile.

"I don't believe you," said Mrs. Wiggins. "But suppose you did. There's two votes for him. Marcus, how many animals promised to vote for you?"

"Well, now—the rats did," said Marcus, twisting his paws and rolling his eyes in embarrassment. "And there was—let me see—"

"You can't tell by asking Marcus," interrupted Grover. "This was a secret vote, and, for all you know, hundreds of animals may want Marcus for president. I must say it looks like it, and although I am surprised, I cannot but accept the fact."

"Yeah," said Jinx, "*you* can accept it if you want to, but *I* won't."

"You'll have to," said Grover calmly. "The animals can vote for whoever they want to."

"That's true," said Freddy suddenly, "and, as a matter of fact, I heard a lot of talk about wanting Georgie for president. I do believe that all these G's I counted for Grover are really votes for Georgie. Three quarters of them, anyway."

Mrs. Wiggins and Jinx nodded solemnly in agreement, and began dividing their G's into two piles. John Quincy and X both began shouting at once, but Grover raised a claw and silenced them.

"Very well," he said. "Count them as you wish. But I shall have nothing further to do with the election.

Come, boys." And he and the two other woodpeckers left the barn.

"I guess he *won't* have anything further to do with the election," said Jinx. "Not if we get an honest count, and not if it keeps on the way it's going. We're 'way ahead so far."

But Simon, who had moved quietly toward a dark corner of the barn, said suddenly: "I protest! I protest against this high-handed action. It is dishonest and unfair, and I shall take the matter before the people of the republic; I shall—"

"You'll take it out of here before I tie a bow knot in your tail," said Jinx, and made a leap for him. But the rat had vanished.

"By gum," said Jinx, staring into the corner, "there's a rat-hole here. Now, when was that done? We had those all stopped up two years ago."

"Simon and his gang have been around a lot lately," said Mrs. Wiggins. "That's one of the first things we have to attend to after election."

"See here, Mrs. Wiggins," said Marcus, "I don't want you to think I had anything to do with this cheating. I just thought it would be fun to run for president, only of course I knew nobody'd vote for me. But then

Simon came to see me, and—well, he made some threats. You know, rats can do a lot of harm to rabbits. So when I found out what they were up to, I didn't dare say anything. But I didn't vote for myself, even. I voted for you—honestly I did."

"Well, well, Marcus," said Mrs. Wiggins comfortably, "I wouldn't worry about that. We don't bear you any ill will. And don't worry about the rats, either. We'll take care of them."

"I'll fix that Simon—you wait," said Marcus, who was beginning to recover his quite unrabbitlike daredevil spirit.

A sudden burst of loud and prolonged cheering made them all look up.

"What's that?" they asked each other. "What's going on?"

And then Bertram's voice boomed out over the barnyard.

"Ladies and gentlemen," he roared, "your new president is—Grover!"

There was another frenzied cheer, and then the voice again. "But there has been trickery. The representatives of the Farmers' Party have deliberately cheated in counting the votes, in order to elect their candidate. Yes, my friends, I know that it is difficult to believe that Mrs. Wiggins would lend her name to such a dishonest and shady transaction. But the facts cannot lie, even if the representatives of the Farmers' Party can."

"Great guns!" said Jinx. "Outside, everybody! We've got to stop this!" And they rushed out into the great crowd of birds and animals that thronged the barnyard.

"But have no fear," Bertram went on. "Your new and duly elected president, Grover, has taken charge. If there is sedition, if there is rebellion, he will put it down with a firm claw."

In the upper doorway of the barn, where Uncle Ben's workshop had been, Bertram was standing, with X and John Quincy perched on his shoulders.

"It's Grover," said Freddy. "He's running Bertram. We've got to get him out of there. Come on."

So Freddy and Jinx and the two dogs ran back into the barn, while Mrs. Wiggins, who couldn't have got up the stairs anyway, stayed in the barnyard to try to quiet the crowd. Her supporters rallied loyally around her, but she was unable to make herself heard by them, for even her loudest voice was not strong enough to overpower Bertram's bellow. In three minutes the two parties had lined up on either side of the barnyard, and it looked as if there was about to be a pitched battle. But Mrs. Wiggins stepped into the open space between them.

I doubt if Mrs. Wiggins ever appeared more truly heroic than at that moment. Ordinarily the most peace-loving of a peace-loving race, when she had pledged herself to a cause which she thought right she was capable of taking a firm stand even in the face of the most determined opposition. Few other cows, I am certain, would have cared to address that angry mob. Fortunately, she was able to address them and be heard, for Bertram was for the moment engaged with the four animals who had run upstairs to attack him.

"Stop!" she shouted. "There must be no fighting. We can settle our differences without that." And then as both sides appeared to be willing at least to hear what she had to say, she began explaining about the votes.

But half-way through her explanation an outburst of barking and an angry screeching came from the loft, and then out through the air sailed Jinx. He landed on his feet beside Mrs. Wiggins, just as the two dogs, snarling and barking angrily, came tumbling down the stairs.

"He's got Freddy!" gasped Robert. "Threw Jinx out of the door and grabbed Freddy and tied him up!"

Just then Bertram came again to the upper door. "Be calm, my friends," he roared. "The welfare of the F.A.R. is still in the hands of its duly elected president. An attempt upon my life, made by certain members of the Farmers' Party, who seem unwilling to abide by the results of our election, has happily been foiled. I have seized the chief conspirator, one Freddy, a pig, and am holding him as hostage for the good behavior of the others."

A roar went up from the barnyard—of applause from one side, of anger from the other.

"But he can't do that!" exclaimed Emma. "Goodness me, it's—it's unheard of!"

"I dunno what Mr. Bean'd say to such goings-on," said Hank. " 'Fraid he'd be dretful angry. Guess I'd better climb them stairs and reason with that bird. Though I dunno's I could get up 'em. Well, I can try."

"Wait, Hank," said Mrs. Wiggins. "Even a horse can't fight Bertram. He's strong as seven horses. We've got to get Grover out of Bertram some way. How did he ever learn to run him?"

"Why, I showed him," said Ronald. "I've showed lots of the animals and birds. We never thought anything like this would happen."

"Of course you didn't," said Robert. "He even

knows that the right arm does funny things, though, for Bertram didn't use it. He tied up Freddy with his left hand."

"Well, we can't fight him," said Mrs. Wiggins. "We'd better talk to Grover and see what he intends to do. Perhaps that will give us some idea of how to get him out of there."

"I'll talk to him with a hoof in the middle of his tail-feathers," said Hank angrily, and the others all looked at him in astonishment. For nobody had ever seen Hank really angry before, even under the most trying circumstances.

"We'll get you your chance," said Mrs. Wiggins dryly. And then turning to the members of the Farmers' Party, she begged them to go quietly to their homes. "When I need you," she said, "I'll send for you. I don't think it will be very long. But in the meanwhile go quietly about your business as you do every day, and above all don't quarrel with anyone on the other side. If we have to fight, we'll fight. But we'll let them start it, and then be ready for them. That's the best policy."

XIV

The interview with Grover was not very satisfactory. In the first place, he insisted that they come up into the loft. "It is my office," he said, "the White House from which I shall govern the F.A.R. If you want to see me, you must come up here. You can hardly expect the president to come to you." And when they pointed out that Mrs. Wiggins could not get up the stairs, he merely remarked that that was too bad.

So Jinx, Robert, Charles, and Henrietta went up.

Grover was still in the control room of Bertram, who received them sitting in Uncle Ben's armchair, with his back to the long bench on which sat Simon and a number of the more important birds who had voted for him. Under the bench, tied tightly, was Freddy. And John Quincy and X sat on Bertram's shoulders.

"Before you begin," said Grover, who had tuned down Bertram's microphone so that his voice was not much louder than it usually was, "I had better tell you what I intend to do. I know what you are going to say, but you don't know what I am going to say. So listen.

"I am the first president of the F.A.R., and I propose to govern the country. You are the heads of the party which opposed my election, and which still opposes it. I do not intend to be hampered in carrying out my plans for the F.A.R. by that opposition, and so I have seized one of you and intend to hold him as hostage for your good behavior. As president, I may point out, I have a perfect right to keep him in prison. As long as you behave yourselves and do as you are told, as long as you obey the laws which I shall pass, Freddy will be kept comfortable and happy. But if you plot against me, if you oppose my commands, he will suffer for it. Do I make myself clear?"

"You do, bug-eater, you do," said Jinx flippantly. "But when you say you're president, you're talking through your hat. Or through Bertram's hat. Bertram's president, not you."

"Have it your own way," said Grover indifferently. "Bertram will punish you if you misbehave. And if you run away, he will punish Freddy."

Jinx scowled for a moment at Bertram, who just sat there motionless, with his left arm resting on one arm of the chair and his right arm—the one that acted up when you tried to work it—hanging down straight over the other. It made Jinx feel queer. Ronald had always run Bertram, and Jinx and the other animals had got to think of the clockwork boy as a real person, and one whom they were fond of. But now he was different. He looked dangerous, and frightening. The woodpeckers, sitting motionless on his shoulders, made him seem strange, too. And the row of birds on the bench, among whom were several hawks and two long-legged, sword-billed herons, made him uncomfortable with their cold stares. Even his old enemy, Simon, whom he had never been afraid of, made him feel nervous.

He looked at his companions. "Nothing we can do now, I guess," he said.

"No," said Robert thoughtfully, "I guess not."

But Henrietta said: "Maybe there's nothing we can do, but there's something I can say. Grover, you're making a fool of yourself. After all, you're nothing but a bird, and like all birds you're vain and silly and headstrong. Oh, I know! I'm a bird myself. You've heard the story about the woodpecker that got hold of the lion's tail and thought it was a worm? Well, that's you. But, as Jinx says, there's nothing we can do now. As a matter of fact, if we do nothing, that's enough. By and by the lion will turn around and bite off your head. Snap! And we'll all go on as we did before you came."

"Thank you, Henrietta," said Grover. "I will remember what you say. But there's one thing more before you go. I want you to know that you will have nothing to lose by behaving yourselves. The laws that will be made will be for your own good. You will be citizens of a greater country than you would ever have been under a president who was nothing but a yokel, like Mrs. Wiggins."

A loud snort from the foot of the stairs made Jinx grin, in spite of his anxiety to get away. Evidently Mrs. Wiggins was listening downstairs.

As they turned to go, Simon said: "Mr. President, hadn't you better tell them yourself about the new orders? They may not believe me."

"Very well," said Grover. And then in a solemn voice he declaimed: "Order number one, issued by me,

• • • Order number one, issued by me • • •

Grover, first president of the F.A.R. Whereas, certain of our citizens have sought redress from me for oppression and maltreatment suffered at the hands of certain other citizens;

"And whereas, their complaint setteth forth that they have been pursued, chased, ignominiously beaten, and deprived of their proper habitations and means of livelihood, and have been housed in miserable dens unfit for citizens of so great a republic;

"And whereas, the conditions as set forth in their complaint have upon investigation been found to be as stated;

"It is hereby ordered that these citizens, namely one Simon, a rat, and his wife, children, and dependents, to the number of twenty-one or more, be hereafter permitted freely to take up residence in any barn or building they may choose, to occupy said premises freely and without molestation under pain of fine and imprisonment;

"And it is further ordered that they be permitted freely, and without let or hindrance, to take for their own use such grain or other food as may be found in said buildings, to an amount not exceeding one peck per rat per day."

Grover stopped and the animals looked at one another again, and Henrietta said: "Now say it all over in English."

"I know what he means," said Robert. "The rats can live in the barn and eat all the grain they want to."

"Come on," said Jinx suddenly. "Let's get out of here before I start chewing my own tail." And he started for the stairs, followed by the others.

In the barn downstairs their friends were waiting for them.

"We heard it all," said Mrs. Wiggins. "Robert, what's a yokel?"

"Search me," said Robert. "But I don't think he meant it as a compliment."

"No," said the cow. "But he's afraid of me or he wouldn't call me names. That's what people always do when they're scared. Well, I'm scared, too, so that makes us even. I'm going home. I want to think. There's nothing we can do now. Grover's got the upper hand, and the thing to do for a while is to go on about our regular business as he told us to. At least we'll pretend to. If anybody thinks of a plan, talk it over with one or two others. We can't hold any big meetings, but we don't need 'em."

"You're our president," said Hank, "and we'll do as you say." And the others all agreed.

That afternoon Grover made a tour of inspection of the farm. With John Quincy and X on his shoulders, Bertram strode rapidly in and out of buildings, and across fields, and through the woods, accompanied by the birds of his staff. The two herons, Eliphalet and Lemuel, whom he had appointed his bodyguard, kept beside him and menaced with their long bills any animals who approached too close. Everywhere he issued orders. Many of the animals who had opposed his election were given extra work, and some were even moved from their homes. Hank had to move out of the barn which had always been his home into the cow-barn, as Grover said the barn was to be used for government offices. Eek and Quik and Eeny and Cousin Augustus also had to leave the barn and move into a hollow tree. Mrs. Wogus and Mrs. Wurzburger were allowed to go about the farm as they always had, but Mrs. Wiggins, whom Grover considered one of his chief enemies, was forbidden to leave the cow-barn on pain of arrest. The chickens had to leave their comfortable chicken-house at ten minutes' notice and move down into the woods. The chicken-house, Grover said, was to be used as barracks for soldiers.

"Soldiers!" said Henrietta. "What are you going to do—start a war?"

"You'll find out," said Grover. "Come. Pack up. You have ten minutes."

And the chickens packed. All the other animals, too, did as they were ordered. It was all they could do, for none of them was strong enough to fight Bertram.

But with old Whibley, Grover struck his first snag. On the tour of inspection, Bertram stopped under the old beech tree and shouted: "Owls! Come out!"

After a minute old Whibley appeared at the entrance of his hole. "Bug-eater again," he said. "Know that voice of yours anywhere. Stepped up with a microphone so it'll sound important. Like wearing high heels to make yourself look taller. Same voice. Little foolisher, if anything."

"Be careful what you say, owl," boomed Bertram. "I come to offer you peace."

"Peace?" said old Whibley. "I can get peace by walking back into my house. Go away, woodpecker."

"Listen," said Bertram. "I am president of the F.A.R. The F.A.R.! A little hill farm, no bigger than half a dozen city blocks! Do you think I am satisfied to be president of a country like that? No! Tomorrow morning my armies will move against Zenas Witherspoon's farm, over the hill. If the Witherspoon animals agree to join the F.A.R., well and good. If they prefer to fight, it will, I assure you, be a very short war. We shall take them in. Then we shall march on the Macy farm, across the valley. And so on. Within three months every animal in New York State will be a citizen of the F.A.R. Within a year, or two at the most, I see a great republic of animals, stretching from coast to coast, a far-flung empire—"

"Far-flung dishwater!" snapped old Whibley. "Never heard such nonsense!"

"Wait," said Bertram. "I have come to offer you a high honor, a position in the government under me. We need brains—"

"I'll say you do," put in the owl.

"We need brains like yours," went on Bertram. "You could rise high, do great things—"

"Stop it!" interrupted the owl. "I can rise high enough without your help. You mean well, Grover. There's just one thing wrong. Mrs. Wiggins is president of the F.A.R.—not you. Go back to your bugs— leave the country to her. She knows more about it than you ever will." And he went back into his hole.

Bertram stood still for a moment. Then he raised his left arm and pointed. "Go bring him out."

Three big hawks swooped from the branches on which they had been sitting, circled, and flew toward the tree, and the two herons, with much flapping of wings, managed to get to branches from which they could reach into the hole with their foot-long beaks. But the owl didn't wait for them. Followed by his niece, Vera, he burst out of the hole, dodged around a tree trunk away from the hawks, and, coming up behind Lemuel, gave him a blow with his powerful wing that knocked the heron squawking from the branch. At the same time Vera swooped expertly through a tangle of branches and dropped on the other heron, who, before he could even get his bill into position to strike, got a crack on the head from her strong curved beak that made him shut his eyes and cling to his perch desperately. And then the owls turned on the hawks.

Neither hawks nor herons can maneuver well in thick woods. The light is dim, and they are not accustomed to diving and swooping among thick foliage. The herons, indeed, had already given up, for their gangling legs and long beaks caught on twigs and got wedged between branches until they hardly dared move. The hawks kept it up for a time, pursuing an enemy whom they seldom even caught a glimpse of, yet who seemed able, somehow, to be far in front of them one moment, and the next to be snatching a beakful of feathers from their wings or tail, or pouncing and ripping painfully with sharp talons.

And all the time old Whibley laughed his hooting laughter.

Grover, peering out of the little window in Bertram's chest, ground his bill in anger. The hawks were brave, he knew. They would fight until they dropped. But he knew too that he couldn't afford to have three of his best fighters in the hospital if there was to be a battle tomorrow. So at last he called them off.

They came down and perched beside him, ruffled, panting, and bedraggled. And Vera and old Whibley perched above them, with hardly a feather out of place.

"Haven't had so much fun in years," said old Whibley. "Must thank you, bug-eater, for providing such good entertainment."

"You wait!" was all Grover could say. "You wait!"

"Not going to," said the owl. "It's war, Grover, and I'm going to start right in today. Duels are silly, but war—that's something different. Besides, Freddy and Mrs. Wiggins are friends of mine. Look out for yourself, Grover. Especially at night." And he and Vera both laughed their eerie, hooting laughter. Grover shivered and, turning Bertram, marched him out of the woods.

In the meantime Freddy was not enjoying himself

much. He had been untied and taken downstairs and shut in the box stall with three guards: Ezra, Simon's eldest son, and two other rats. The box stall had once been used by the animals as a jail, and escape from it would have been pretty difficult, even if it were left unguarded. But with the rats there, escape was out of the question. They knew what was to be expected from Freddy's friends, and not a mouse could get near the stall.

But the rats had a good time at first. They made up ribald songs about Freddy and sang them. One or two of them were quite funny and even made Freddy laugh. And when they looked at him in surprise, he remembered his belief in the power of laughter and burst into a roar.

"The song isn't as funny as all that," said Ezra doubtfully.

"I'm not laughing at the song," said Freddy. "Just something I thought of."

They pressed him to tell them what it was, but Freddy wouldn't; he just kept on laughing, and by and by the rats got uneasy. They stopped singing and prowled around the stall, peering and listening.

"Aw, it isn't anything," they said at last. "He's just trying to get our goat."

"Sure, boys. That's it," said Freddy seriously. He was sober for a while, and then he began to chuckle as if he just couldn't hold it in.

Before he was through he had the rats so nervous and unstrung that they sent word out, and three other rats took their places. By that time it was six o'clock, and Freddy was hungry. But the rats said orders were that he couldn't have any supper. "Your friend old Whibley has been misbehaving," they said. "So of course you get punished for it."

After that, Freddy didn't feel up to laughing any more, so he curled up and tried to go to sleep.

For a time the tramp of Bertram's heavy footsteps and the sounds of bird and animal voices upstairs, to say nothing of the hunger gnawing in the pit of his stomach, kept him awake. By and by he fell into a doze, and watched a procession of dinners and lunches and breakfasts and bowls of soup and big platters piled high with food passing by, just out of reach. He moaned and tossed about in his sleep, and his guards woke up and grinned at each other.

"Beefsteak, Freddy," whispered one.

"Apple pie," whispered another.

Freddy moaned louder.

"Aw, let him alone," said the third.

It must have been about midnight when Freddy was awakened by a sharp little whisper in his ear. "It's me, Freddy—Webb. Quiet, don't move."

Freddy lay still.

"Listen," said the spider. "We're going to try to rescue you tomorrow while Grover and his army are attacking the Witherspoon farm."

"But you can't!" Freddy exclaimed. "It's too dangerous."

He had forgotten the guards, and now they jumped up and came over to him.

But Freddy remembered in time. He gave a sort of half snore that ended in a moan, and said, as if talking in his sleep: "Take it away, I tell you. Take it away!"

"Hey, Freddy, what's the matter?" said one of the rats, putting a paw on his shoulder.

"Eh? Wh-what? What's wrong?" exclaimed the pig, starting up and looking around wildly. Then he sank back. "What did you want to wake me for!" he said crossly. "I was just finishing a big plate of lobster salad and they were bringing me in a mince pie."

"Guess it's just as well I did, then," said the guard with a laugh. "All right, boys. He was just dreaming."

When everything had quieted down, Mr. Webb

said: "I can't tell you the whole plan now, for there's lots to do and I must get back. But you be ready. When you're out, we can decide what to do about Grover. And, by the way, don't worry about the bank. Grover stopped there on his tour of inspection today and said that he supposed it was up to him to take charge of it, since the bank president was in jail. So he put X in charge of it. But John went down there just after they grabbed you this noon, and he dug another room and moved all the money and valuables into it, and then he closed it up so nobody would know where it was. Grover is planning to use that money, I think, but he'll never find it now. Well, so long." And Mr. Webb dropped down to the floor and tiptoed across it and up the wall and through a crack over the window to safety.

Freddy felt a lot better in his mind, but a lot worse in his stomach, for he was getting hungrier and hungrier. He couldn't sleep, and there was no use trying to figure out how his friends planned to rescue him, so he decided to annoy the rats. And he suddenly gave a loud laugh.

The rats jumped up, squeaking excitedly, and rushed over to him. "What is it? What goes on? What's the matter?"

Freddy blinked at them. "Oh, sorry, boys. Guess I must have had a nightmare."

"A laughing nightmare!" said one incredulously.

"Sure," said Freddy. "I often have 'em. Specially when I have something on my mind. Something funny, I mean."

"Perhaps if you told us what it was, you wouldn't have any more of them," said the second guard.

"Perhaps," said Freddy. "Good night, boys." And he turned over.

Freddy had six more laughing nightmares during the night, each louder and more startling than the last. The three rats were wrecks by morning.

X V

Grover's army marched at dawn. They filed out of the gate and up the road toward the Witherspoon farm, Bertram in the lead, with John Quincy and X on his shoulders and the two herons stalking beside him; then in a not very orderly column came a regiment of wood rats, weasels, and other small animals, with a mercenary dog or two. Overhead the sky was empty of birds. The three hawks were scouting ahead of the column, but the main body of birds was not to start until Bertram entered the Witherspoon farmyard. The rats had been left behind to garrison the Bean farm. Of course the Farmers' Party could easily rise and overwhelm the rats, but Grover felt sure that they would not dare do anything for which they would be certain to be punished severely on his return.

The army marched over the hill and poured into the Witherspoon farmyard, just as the birds, flying in four columns high in the air, came into sight. Mrs. Witherspoon was looking out the window, for although she never went anywhere, she seldom missed anything that was going on outside.

But she had never seen anything like this before. She pushed her spectacles up on her forehead so she could see better, and then she threw up the window and called out: "Boy! You—boy! What do you want?"

Bertram saluted her and said: "Madam, nobody is going to harm you. Just stay inside the house and everything will be all right."

"Well, I'm certainly not coming out for you," said Mrs. Witherspoon. "If you want Mr. Witherspoon, I don't know where he is." And having given this useful piece of information, she slammed down the window and went back to her work. For she had a good deal to do. She was not a very fast worker, and she was still finishing putting up last season's preserves.

Two dogs ran out of the barn, barking.

"Dogs," said Bertram, "go call together all the animals and birds on this farm. We have come to annex it in the name of the president of the F.A.R."

"Yeah?" said the dogs, and they rushed at Bertram, and one of them bit him in the left leg, and the other bit him in the right. And then they both let go and yelped and retreated to a safe distance. For of course Bertram's legs were wood.

Mr. Zenas Witherspoon heard the racket and came out of the barn, where he had been playing solitaire. He had a passion for solitaire, and that was one reason why he could not make his farm pay and why he hadn't been able to buy shoes for his horse, Jerry. He spent a lot of the time when he should have been plowing or milking or pitching hay in trying to make solitaire games come out.

"What's all this?" asked Mr. Witherspoon.

Bertram explained courteously. "We aren't going to interfere with you," he said. "You will run your farm just as before. We are organizing the animals into a republic, but they will continue to work for you. The only difference will be that in animal affairs they will owe allegiance to the F.A.R. They will be called upon occasionally for military duty, and will give part of their food to help feed the army. There will be a distinct advantage to you, for it is to the interest of the

F.A.R. to see that the farms forming its subject states are well and properly run."

"Well," said Mr. Witherspoon, who was anxious to get back to his solitaire game, "guess that's for them to decide, then." And he went back into the barn.

By this time the Witherspoon animals had all gathered and were looking with amazement at Bertram and his army and the scores of birds that perched in rows on the roofs and branches.

Then Bertram made a speech. He told of the founding of the F.A.R., and of his plan for a great empire of animals. He talked for an hour, and many of the Witherspoon animals became enthusiastic and were all for joining. But Jerry and a cow named Eunice and one or two others were not convinced.

"I don't know as we want to join," said Jerry. "We're satisfied here. We don't want to be in any army. We don't want glory and we aren't heroes— we're just plain animals. I guess you can just count us out."

"I shan't argue with you," said Bertram. "If at the end of two minutes you still refuse to join us, I shall tear down your cow-barn."

Some of the animals looked frightened, but Jerry only laughed. "Go ahead," he said.

"Look," said Bertram. He walked over to a fence-post which was sunk deep in the ground, seized it with his left hand, gave a preliminary tug, and pulled it out. "Now do you think I can tear down your barn?" he said.

The animals talked together for a moment. Then Jerry stepped forward. "I guess we'll have to join," he said sullenly. "We can't have things pulled to pieces. All right; we agree."

"Good," said Bertram. "In the name of the F.A.R. I take possession of this farm, which will be known hereafter as the sovereign State of Witherspoonia. And now I will give you my orders."

Back in his dungeon, Freddy was waiting impatiently for the expected rescue to take place. "I wish they'd hurry," he kept saying to himself. "I hope they won't forget to bring something to eat." He had been quite faint from hunger when he woke that morning. Not that that was anything unusual. He often got faint from hunger when he missed one of his usual half-hourly snacks. The rats had brought him a cabbage and three raw turnips for breakfast—not exactly a banquet, as he pointed out. But they just laughed. And so he sat and longed for food and freedom.

But at last something did happen. Through the

crack by the window, which Mr. Webb had used the night before, a wasp came crawling. It was Jacob. Freddy saw him before the guards did, and Jacob waved a reassuring feeler at him and then motioned him to be quiet. In single file ten wasps with drawn stings crawled through after their leader and lined up on the ledge over the window. Then at a signal they dove upon the unsuspecting rats.

There was a great squealing and scrabbling, but there was no cover in the box stall—none, that is, except Freddy. In five seconds the three terrified rats had crawled in under the prisoner, like chickens taking refuge beneath their mother's wing.

Out in the other part of the barn Freddy could hear scampering and squeaking, and he judged that another body of wasps was taking care of the rats left in charge of the farm by Grover.

Jacob lit close to Freddy's ear. "I guess the coast is clear," he whispered. "I hear Hank coming to unbar the door. As soon as you're out, run for the cow-barn. Mrs. Wiggins will tell you what to do next."

"I certainly appreciate this, Jacob," said the grateful pig. "I won't forget it."

"Pooh!" said the wasp. "Any of your friends could have driven the rats off. But it's better for us to do it, for Grover'll have a hard time arresting us. We tried to get Grover this morning; there's a crack in Bertram's neck where a wasp can just get through. But boy, have those herons got sharp eyes! And beaks! We didn't have a chance. So we tried this way. Well, here's Hank. We'll take care of these three lads when you get up. Herd 'em down to the pond, I guess. A bath'll do 'em good."

The box-stall door opened and Freddy ran out and found Hank waiting. The barn was empty except for a dozen cruising wasps. "Hurry," said the horse, and they ran for the cow-barn. Outside, a shadow swept across the barnyard, and Freddy looked up. In broad daylight a great owl was floating noiselessly past. "It's old Whibley," said Hank. "He and Vera have cleared the air for us. They've driven down every bird left on the farm. There won't be anybody to tell Grover where you went."

In the cow-barn no time was wasted. "Georgie went over to the pigpen and got that disguise you wore to the orphan asylum last year," said Mrs. Wiggins. "Slip into it quick, Freddy, and get away before Grover gets back. There's some money in the shopping bag. John got that from the bank. I guess the best plan would be to go to Centerboro for a while. We'll keep in touch with you through Jacob."

The disguise was an old gingham dress of Mrs. Bean's, a sunbonnet into which were pinned two long corkscrew curls, a pair of black lace mitts, and a shopping bag with a picture of the Bridge of Sighs on it. The dress, like all Freddy's disguises, was too long, and he had torn off part of the front hem so that he could walk in it without falling on his nose. It didn't improve its appearance any.

Mrs. Wiggins shook her head doubtfully when he had at last struggled into it. "I don't know, Freddy. Except for being about fifty years behind the times, it's a good costume. And it hides everything but the end of your nose. And yet it doesn't hide the most important fact about you."

"And what's that?" said Freddy, tying his bonnet strings under his chin.

"That you're a pig, of course," said Jinx. "Just take a word of advice, Freddy. Don't go to the butcher's house for tea while you're leading the gay life in Centerboro."

"Instead of passing all these wisecracks," said Freddy, "you might be getting me something to eat.

I'm practically starving. Look at this dress. Last year I could hardly get into it, and now it hangs on me like a sack."

"Well, you wanted to reduce," said Robert. "Maybe we ought to have left you in jail. Just think what a fine figure you'd have after a month of bread and water."

Freddy merely grunted and, drawing the lace mitts over his fore trotters, dropped a curtsy to his friends and walked out into the barnyard. A quick look around assured him that no one was in sight, and he walked quickly out of the gate and took the road for Centerboro.

Mrs. Wiggins looked after him and shook her head again. "I don't know," she said. "There's something about a pig . . . I wonder what it can be."

It wasn't a very long walk to Centerboro; but for a pig in a gingham dress and a sunbonnet, on a hot spring day, it was quite a trip. Particularly for a hungry pig. Once beyond the Bean farm, Freddy began waving to every car that passed him in the hope of getting a ride. But the occupants merely waved back and went on, laughing heartily.

"Something's wrong," said Freddy. "I wish Mrs. Wiggins cared a little more about her looks; she'd have had a mirror in the cow-barn. Of *course* I can't get a

208

disguise on properly if I can't see myself in a mirror."

He walked on a half-mile or so and met a little girl.

"Hello, pig," said the little girl, whose name was Genevieve Stamp. I don't know why I tell you her name, for she doesn't come into the story again. But maybe you'd like to know it.

"What!" said Freddy severely, speaking in a high falsetto which he had put on with the disguise. "Little girl, that is no way to address your elders."

"But you *are* a pig," said Genevieve.

"When I was a little girl like you—" Freddy began.

But Genevieve started to giggle. "You weren't *just* like me," she said.

"Perhaps not *just*," said Freddy. "But, at any rate, I was a little girl and now I am an old lady, and when you get to be my age—"

"Tee-hee!" said the little girl, giggling worse than ever. "I never saw an old lady before with a little curly tail."

"What!" said Freddy, and he looked over his shoulder and saw that, sure enough, his tail was sticking out through the placket of the gingham dress. "Good grief! Now how did that get there?"

"I guess it grew there," said the little girl, and she ran off, laughing merrily.

So Freddy tucked the tail in, and the next car he waved to drew up beside him. Freddy could not see the driver, for he had to keep his head down so that the sunbonnet would hide his face, but there was something familiar about the voice that said: "Deary me, madam, this is a great pleasure to be sure. Get in, get in."

Freddy tripped on the skirt getting in and fell in a heap at the man's feet, but he managed to scramble up and into the seat before his sunbonnet fell off.

He settled himself with great dignity.

"Now this is very good of you," he said, "to give an old lady a lift. I take it very kindly of you."

"*Old* lady, did you say, madam?" inquired the man gallantly. "Why, you're no older than my daughter, I'll be bound."

"Oh, sir," said Freddy with a giggle, "I fear you are a great flatterer. And a great ladies' man, I can see with half an eye." And as the car had started again, and the man was certainly watching the road, Freddy risked half an eye under his sunbonnet and saw, as he had expected, that his companion was the little man with a face like a pig's, who had been wandering about the Bean farm.

"Are you going far, ma'am?" the man inquired.

• • • Good grief! How did that get there? • • •

Freddy thought a moment. He remembered the man's mysterious interest in the Beans, and especially in the First Animal Bank, and now, he saw, was his chance to exercise his undoubted ability as a detective and find out what the fellow was up to.

"Sure," he said, becoming suddenly very Irish, "I'm for Centerboro, and the fine big bank there, for I have a little business to transact. And indeed I'd better be introducin' meself, what with you bein' so kind and all. I'm Mrs. O'Halloran, from Dutchman's Meadows, down beyond the Bean place, where all the smart animals live."

"Deary me, and I'm pleased to meet you, Mrs. O'Halloran," said the man. "And I am Jason Binks, without any very pressing business on my hands today, and so shan't we take a little ride around and have a look at the countryside this pretty spring day?"

"Sure, why wouldn't I jump at the chance," said Freddy, shaking his curls coquettishly, "to ride about in a great luxurious motor-car with a fine handsome man like yourself? 'Tis not pressin', my business at the bank, being only to transfer me little savin's from this bank the animals do be runnin' on the Bean farm to a better place."

"Now that's odd," said Mr. Binks. "Deary me,

that's odd as odd! You don't like the animal bank, I take it?"

"Indeed," said Freddy, "and how would anybody be havin' respect for a bank or likin' for it that's housed in an old shed with birds flyin' in and out the windows and cows and dogs and horses trampin' in and out and a pig sittin' behind the counter and askin' your business? And chargin' a poor old widow woman a cent a month to keep her wee bagful of pennies safe for her. And not so safe either, if it's all so what they're sayin'."

"Dear, dear, what a dreadful place! And what are they saying, Mrs. O'Halloran?"

"They do be sayin', Mr. Binks, that that pig that runs the bank, bad cess to him, is a dreadful great scoundrel. 'Twas him I saw this mornin', and 'twas only my threat to bring the law down on him that made him give up my money. ' 'Tis safe here, Mrs. O'Halloran,' says he. 'Why don't you leave it lay?' 'Why don't I leave it lay, is it?' says I. 'I'll tell you why, Mr. Freddy,' I says. ' 'Twas Mr. Bean, the good man, got me to put my money here, but what help would Mr. Bean be to me now, and him away, and you animals doin' what you please with the money? I'd not trust you,' I says, 'as far as I could throw a bull by the tail, and that,' I says, 'ain't any distance at all.' "

"Good for you, Mrs. O'Halloran," said Mr. Binks, giving two toots on his horn to show his approval. "But this pig, now—he's dishonest, I think you said?"

"Ah, 'tis kind of you, so it is, to listen to the troubles of a poor old body. A heart of gold you have, Mr. Binks, and I'll say it to your face. But here's the whole countryside full of beautiful scenery, and us talkin' trouble. We'll have no more of it."

"Ah, but this Freddy, now," said Mr. Binks, "this naughty little piggy. Somehow, Mrs. O'Halloran, I can't think he's so very bad. Have you really any proof of it?"

"Enough is enough," said Freddy. "Would you look at those big maples, now, and them so beautiful against the sky?"

"They're elms, I think," said Mr. Binks, "but still beautiful, of course. Well, Mrs. O'Halloran, I see I must tell you more. For I am interested in this animal bank—oh, yes, very much indeed. I am, in short, a detective."

"A detective!" Freddy exclaimed. "Are you so! Well now, many's the time I've thought I'd like well to be a detective, and go about among folk in false whiskers and disguises and worm their secrets out of them."

Mr. Binks laughed heartily. "We don't use disguises any more, ma'am," he said. "Dear me, no. Disguises are not much use in our line. And you'll excuse me, ma'am, but I'm sure you could never deceive anybody, for you're too honest and open and unpracticed in following clues. No, no, ma'am; nobody could ever take you for anything but what you are: a charming and honest Irish lady."

"Sure, you put me to the blush, Mr. Binks, so you do," said Freddy, "though it's not without charm you are yourself, as well you know. Go on with you, Mr. Binks." And Freddy tapped him playfully on the arm.

Mr. Binks cackled delightedly and, changing the subject, began to talk of the beauties of nature. But Freddy noticed that he had turned back toward Centerboro, and a few minutes later they drew up before the imposing front of the Centerboro National Bank.

"Why, deary me!" said Mr. Binks in a surprised tone. "Here we are in Centerboro, to be sure! And right in front of the bank. Well now, Mrs. O'Halloran, why not go in, since we're here, and deposit your savings? And then, if you would care to, I should like to have you meet my friend Mr. Henry Weezer, the bank's president."

XVI

Freddy did not know how much money John had put into the shopping bag, but he was getting hungrier and hungrier, and he thought, however much it was, he would have to spend all of it for things to eat. He certainly wasn't going to pretend it was Mrs. O'Halloran's savings and put it in the bank. So he told Mr. Binks that he would like to meet Mr. Weezer first.

"For 'tis not every day I could be hobnobbin' with a bank president," he said, "and the rest can wait."

So Mr. Binks took him right into Mr. Weezer's office.

"Mr. Weezer," he said, "I'd like you to meet a friend of mine, Mrs. O'Halloran. She's bringing her savings over from the First Animal to deposit them here, and I thought you might like to talk to her. They haven't used her very well over there."

Mr. Weezer got up and shook hands. He looked a little surprised when he shook Freddy's fore trotter, and he looked down at it curiously, but the black lace mitt concealed the fact that it was not really a hand at all.

"I am sorry to hear that they treated you badly," he said. "What was the trouble, madam?"

"Ah, sir," said Freddy, "the rascals! And that great murderin' ruffian of a pig that's president!"

"Yes, yes," said Mr. Weezer anxiously. "Did they steal some of your money?"

"Not to say steal exactly, sir. But they'd not give it up until I threatened to have the law of them."

"Dear, dear," said Mr. Weezer. "This is not the first time I have heard of something like this. It is time something was done about it. Would you be willing now, madam, to make a complaint against them to the authorities?"

"Ah, sure," said Freddy, "what good's complaints, savin' your honor's presence. And they'll not be trou-

217

blin' me more, now my money's under your honor's protection."

"That is true," said the president. "But I will be frank with you, Mrs. O'Halloran. I have already complained to the authorities myself about this animal bank. I do not believe, myself, that animals are fit to take care of other people's money. But there was nothing the authorities could do. As long as the bank was run properly, they couldn't close it down. However, they said that if a complaint came in from some depositor who had actually been dishonestly treated by the bank, they would act. I'll be frank with you. I have not up to now been able to find such a person. Most of the bank's clients are animals, and I do not believe that the authorities would pay much attention to a complaint from a squirrel or a horse. But if you, madam—"

"No, your honor," interrupted Freddy. "Not me, *if* you please. I'd like well to be even with that Freddy, and true I did threaten to have the law of him. But I'd not be callin' the police, for I don't like the police too well, and that's the truth."

"H'm," said Mr. Weezer, and he frowned at Mr. Binks.

So Freddy said: "H'm." He would have said it twice, just to go Mr. Weezer one better, but the first

"H'm" sounded rather too much like a pig's grunt. So he let it go at one "H'm" and thought a minute. Then he said: "Your honor, ye've said twice: 'I'll be frank with you, Mrs. O'Halloran.' 'Twas a promise ye've not kept, but now I'm askin' you to keep it. Why do you want to put the animal bank out of business?"

"I assure you, madam—" Mr. Weezer began, but Mr. Binks said:

"Deary me, I think Mrs. O'Halloran is a friend." And he nodded emphatically at Mr. Weezer.

"Well, to be entirely frank—" said the president.

"Never mind the frankness," said Freddy. "Do you just be tellin' me the truth."

So Mr. Weezer said: "It's simply a matter of business, madam. If the animal bank was really an animal bank, I would have no quarrel with it. But it has taken from me one of my best clients, Mr. Bean. And as soon as other farmers in the country hear about it, I am afraid that they too will deposit their money in the animal bank. And what will happen? If it keeps on, the First National Bank of Centerboro will have to close its doors."

"So that's it!" said Freddy. "Thank ye, sir, for doin' a poor old woman the honor of tellin' her the truth. And I suppose you've hired this detective felly to poke around and find ye somebody that'll make a complaint?"

"That is so. But I must say he has not been of much help. For you're the first one he's found, and now you say you won't do it." And he looked sourly at Mr. Binks, who blushed faintly and said:

"Well, deary me, if you'd only taken my advice—"

"No," said Mr. Weezer firmly. "I do not like the animal bank, but I will not use dishonest methods against it. I leave it to you, Mrs. O'Halloran. Mr. Binks thinks that we should go up to the First Animal some night with a pick and shovel and dig into the vaults and take all the money and bring it down here. Then of course when Mr. Bean wants his money, it will not be there, and he will make the First Animal close up. Afterwards we can turn the money over to Mr. Bean, explaining that it was found somewhere or other. Don't you agree that the First National should refuse to enter into any such dishonest transaction?"

"Why, Mr. Binks!" Freddy exclaimed. "Sure, it's surprised at you I am, and you so open an' honest-lookin'!"

"Well, ma'am—" began Mr. Binks, turning this time very red.

"Well ma'am me no well ma'am's," said Freddy severely. (And if you think it is an easy thing to say, just try it.) "Out upon you, sir! Fie!"

Mr. Binks seemed to get smaller, and he wiped his forehead and muttered something. But Freddy turned to Mr. Weezer.

"Often and often," he said, "I've heard Mr. Bean praisin' the honesty and goodness of bankers, 'and particularly,' he says, 'Mr. Weezer of the First National. Now, there,' he says, 'is an upright man.' No, no, Mr. Weezer; 'tis indeed hard to have this animal bank takin' away your business, but 'tis not to be corrected by skulduggery. But now what would you say, sir, if I was to tell you that I could shut down the First Animal without any finaglin' or skulduggery at all?"

"You, madam?" said Mr. Weezer, and he started to smile his thin little smile, and then decided better not, for who knew?—perhaps this funny old woman could really do something for him. He had better find out. So he said: "If you could do it, madam, there is scarcely anything you could not ask in return."

"Ah, then," said Freddy, "I'll have to be thinkin' up somethin' to ask, for I'll tell ye, sir, I'm as sure of bein' able to do it as I am that my name's Bridget O'Halloran.—Surer," he added after a second.

"Then I shall not need your services any longer,"

said Mr. Weezer to Mr. Binks. "Good afternoon, sir. Mr. Horgly will give you your pay." And Mr. Binks went out muttering.

"Now, madam," said Mr. Weezer.

But Freddy shook his head. He could not, he said, arrange to do as he had promised immediately. Mr. Weezer must give him a few days. Within the week, he gave his word, he would drop in at the bank and they could arrange matters. Mr. Weezer argued and argued, but Freddy was firm. He had to be firm because he didn't know yet what he was going to ask Mr. Weezer to do for him in return. And at last Mr. Weezer gave in.

"Very well," he said. "If I must wait, then I must wait. But about your savings, madam—wouldn't you like to deposit them here for safekeeping?" And when Freddy said unwillingly: "Yes," Mr. Weezer said: "And how large a sum is it, may I ask?"

Freddy looked in the shopping bag. There were three quarters and a nickel and a penny. "Eighteen cents," he said.

And for the first and only time in his life Mr. Weezer's glasses fell off at the mention of a sum under ten dollars. He put them back on his nose and stared at Freddy in amazement. "Your entire life savings?" he exclaimed. "Only—" Then he stopped himself. After all, the amount didn't matter, though that was certainly the smallest amount for the entire life savings of a very old woman that he had ever heard of. So they went out and Freddy deposited the money, leaving only sixty-three cents in the shopping bag.

When this was done, Mr. Weezer, who didn't want to lose sight of the only person who had shown any signs of being able to help the First National out of its difficulties, invited Freddy to lunch. But hungry as the pig was—and by now he really was beginning to feel a little faint—he refused. It wouldn't do now for Mr. Weezer to find out what he was, and although he had very good table manners, and didn't eat like a pig, he was afraid he might look like a pig when he ate. There is really quite a difference. Besides, he had to get away and think. So he said good-by to Mr. Weezer and went off down the street.

Next door to the bank there was a small restaurant called Ye Tidy Tea Shoppe. A bill of fare was pasted in the window, and Freddy stopped to look at it. As he looked, delicious smells puffed out of the restaurant door and up his nose, which wiggled eagerly in spite of him. Lunch was thirty cents, and he was just turning in when Mr. Weezer's voice at his shoulder said:

"Very good food they have here. Come along in with me, Mrs. O'Halloran, do."

Freddy gulped. "No—no, thank you kindly, sir. I couldn't eat a bite." And he went on.

In a bakery down the street he bought some doughnuts and some buns and sat on a bench in the park and ate them, and then he felt better. While he was sitting there he saw several birds, among them a hawk, circling and wheeling above the town, and he knew they were some of Grover's scouts, looking for him. But he felt perfectly safe.

He didn't have enough money to stay at the hotel, so he went around to see the sheriff, who was a friend of his, and got permission to sleep in the barn. He told the sheriff he was working as a detective, on a case, so the sheriff didn't ask any questions, but took him to a ball game, and after that to the movies, and when Freddy finally got to bed that night in the sheriff's haymow, he was so full of peanuts and popcorn and chocolate bars which the sheriff had bought him that he could hardly get out of the gingham dress.

XVII

When Grover and his army got back after the conquest and annexation of Witherspoonia, scouts were sent out in all directions to find Freddy. But no trace of him could be found. And as nobody but the wasps seemed to have had anything to do with his escape, Grover had no one to punish.

He didn't particularly want to punish anybody, anyway. His first day in office had, he felt, been highly successful. He had added a state to the F.A.R. The country was quiet—even the members of the Farmers' Party seemed resigned to his rule. Old Whibley and Vera, it is true, with Ferdinand and a small band of the robber crows who had not gone home after voting for Mrs. Wiggins, waged a sort of guerrilla warfare on his government, swooping out from their stronghold in the woods to attack his army, or to drive from their nests the birds whom he had brought in to vote for him. But old Whibley, Grover felt, could be attended to later.

During the next few days, while Freddy was spending most of his time in the sheriff's barn in Centerboro, trying to think out some scheme for bringing Mrs. Wiggins back into power, the armies of the F.A.R. carried a lightning campaign through the valley, annexing in quick succession the states of Macia, Smithia, Johnsonia, Winterbottomia, and Bodgettia. They fought only one battle, when the Winterbottom animals, led by an old circus horse named Charlie, learned in advance of their march and tried to trap them in a narrow ravine on Wigwam Creek. Charlie had planned to ambush them and roll rocks down on them, but a squadron of meadowlarks, scouting in advance of the column, discovered the ambush in time. Grover altered the course of his march, came upon the enemy from the rear, and, instead of the rocks, a number of the Winterbottom animals rolled to the bottom of the ravine before the rest surrendered and submitted to annexation.

Each afternoon, after the return of the army, Grover held court in the loft of the barn. He—or rather Bertram—sat in Uncle Ben's chair, with John Quincy on one shoulder and X on the other, and the two herons behind him. On the long work-bench sat the members of his staff. Here Bertram gave out orders, and made laws, and handed down judgments. It was here that Charlie and two of his lieutenants were sentenced to six months' imprisonment.

But though the Farmers' Party seemed to have resigned itself to Grover's overlordship, there was a good deal of undercover activity going on. Nearly every night Jinx and John and the dogs and some of the chickens sneaked into the cow-barn, where they held muttered conferences with the cows and Hank. Sometimes old Whibley came for a moment, to report progress, and every night Jacob brought messages from Freddy, whom he visited every day. A great many plans had been proposed, but none of them were very good. And they all felt that when they finally took action, the plan they acted upon must be perfect.

Freddy, in the meanwhile, had been eating, and thinking. About as much of the one as of the other, for the sheriff set a good table. But the more he ate, the fatter he got, and the fatter he got, the better he felt, and the better he felt, the clearer he could think. And at last he thought of something.

He put on the gingham dress and the bonnet and the curls and the mitts and set off for the bank.

"Good morning, Mrs. O'Halloran," said Mr. Weezer.

"Good mornin' to you, sir," said Freddy. "I've come to do business with you."

"Good," said Mr. Weezer.

" 'Tis an agreement I want from you, Mr. Weezer," said Freddy. "You'll agree that the day the First Animal makes a rule that it will take no more business from anybody but an animal or a bird, you will do certain things."

"Ah," said Mr. Weezer, "and what are the things?"

So Freddy told him, and after a little argument Mr. Weezer agreed. And he wrote out the agreement and signed it. And when Freddy had folded it up and tucked it away in the shopping bag, he took off his sunbonnet.

Mr. Weezer's mouth and eyes flew open as if they had little springs in them, and his glasses didn't fall off—they jumped. And he said: "A pig!"

"Yes, sir," said Freddy. "And very glad not to have to talk that Irish stuff any more, for it was beginning to get the best of me, and if it had gone on much longer, I would never have been able to talk anything else."

Mr. Weezer leaned down and brushed up the fragments of his glasses from the floor and threw them into the wastebasket.

"I'm sorry about the glasses," said Freddy.

"They're only window glass," said Mr. Weezer. "As a matter of fact, I can see better without them. I only wear them because it makes me look more like a bank president."

"I never thought of that," said Freddy. "I shall have to get a pair. That is, if the First Animal stays in business."

"What!" said Mr. Weezer. "You are Freddy, the president of the First Animal? The famous detective? Of course, I might have known."

"You might," said Freddy, "but you didn't. And now, as one bank president to another, and to be perfectly frank with you, I don't want to injure the First National, and from now on the First Animal will do business only with animals. And now for your part of the contract."

So Mr. Weezer sat down and wrote the following letter:

Hon. Grover
President First Animal Republic
Bean Farm, N.Y.
Honored Sir:

Having learned of the magnificent project which you have recently undertaken, and of the glorious victories of your armies, on which I heartily congratulate you, I take the liberty of writing to ask if you will do me the favor of calling on me at my home tomorrow evening, Friday, at eight o'clock. Knowing that you are a banker of wide experience, there are several matters which I should like to discuss with you. I need hardly point out that in waging a war of conquest, it is important to have the bankers on your side. I am on your side, respected sir, but in order to be practically useful, I feel that we should come to an agreement.

Awaiting your esteemed reply, I am,
Yours respectfully,
Henry Q. Weezer
President, First National Bank
of Centerboro

The letter was sent at once by messenger, and half an hour later a starling flew in the bank window carrying Grover's reply in his beak. Mr. Weezer opened it and spread it out on the table. It had been written on Freddy's typewriter, and there were a good many mistakes in it, for Freddy was the only animal on the farm who could use a typewriter. But it speaks very well for Grover, I think, that he had been able to type it at all.

> mR. Hen!yQW₃3zer
> president Frst Nat.Bank
> centerboro
> Inreply to yours of eveb date
> wish   tolstate#I SHall
> be plexscd to waitt on/you
> at ¢ at $ at 8 o(clok onevening
> of FRIDAY MAY *—may @¢
> may *!₃!"   i will bethere
>   Grover   President FAR

"Good!" said Freddy. "I thought he'd come. I expect he was pretty thrilled to be asked to call on a real banker in his home. Well, now for our arrangements." He put on his bonnet and hurried back to the sheriff's barn, where Jacob was waiting to carry his instructions to the farm.

XVIII

Mr. Henry Weezer lived at 125 Winker Street in Centerboro. Mrs. Eliza Blench, who lived at No. 124, across the street, and who always wrote down in her diary whatever she saw going on through her front parlor window curtains, was kept pretty busy that Friday. She wrote so fast and furiously that by nine o'clock in the evening she ran out of ink and had to go upstairs and borrow some from her boarder, Mr. Wilfred Attlebury. But by the time she got back, everything was all over.

Some of the entries in Mrs. Blench's diary have

nothing to do with our story, such as the one at 9.15 a.m., about the little Linderman boy falling off his velocipede, and though interesting enough if we only had time for them, I shall have to leave them out. But here are some that she wrote down about No. 125:

8.30 a.m. Mr. Weezer left for the bank. Looked worried.

9.05. Boy from Lieber & Wingus delivered large fire-extinguisher at Weezer's.

10.15. Old lady in sunbonnet let herself in Weezer's front door with key. Query: new housekeeper?

11.04. Large swarm of wasps on Weezer's front porch.

11.20. Wasps all flew in through open window. Must warn Mr. W.

12 m. Very strange thing has just happened. Two roosters came down the street, stopped in front of Weezer's, looked at the house, then flew in through parlor window.

1.33. Queerer and queerer. Two large birds just flew in W.'s parlor window. If I had ever seen an owl, I should say they were owls.

2.05. Called up Mr. Weezer at the bank and told him about owls and roosters. Also wasps. Offered to go over and shoo them out. Was told politely to mind my own business. Hope he gets good and stung.

3.15. I simply cannot understand this at all. An old white horse just came down the street, climbed up on Mr. Weezer's porch, and rang the front doorbell with his hoof. Was admitted by little old woman, still wearing her sunbonnet. Before the door was closed, a cat and two dogs dashed around the house and in after the horse.

4.25. Just back from Dr. Payne's. He says my glasses don't need changing. Says my eyes are all right. Didn't tell him about horse.

5.04. Horse just looked out of W.'s parlor window. Saw me, and grinned and waved hoof at me.

At this point Mrs. Blench's writing becomes so bad, and her words so confused, that the diary is too hard to read. But it is plain that all day long, by ones and twos, the animals had been sneaking away from the farm and gathering at Mr. Weezer's. Mostly, of course, the small animals; for the absence of the bigger ones would have been noticed by Grover. Mrs. Wiggins and the others hadn't really wanted Hank to go, but he had insisted, and as Hank rarely insisted on

234

· · · · admitted by little old woman · · ·

anything, they thought it better to humor him. It was easy enough for Hank, anyway, for he had some plowing to do in one of the upper lots, and it was not noticeable when he slipped out of his harness and trotted off toward Centerboro.

Grover, indeed, didn't notice anything at all. At the head of an army which now, with all the new farms he had added to the F.A.R., was nearly three times as large as it had been at first, he returned from a forced march of six miles to annex three small hill farms, and late in the afternoon held his usual court in the loft over the barn. He was in very high spirits. For an invitation to call on the most important banker in the county wasn't something that everybody got. Probably no woodpecker before him had ever been so honored. That there might be danger in going never even crossed his mind. Bertram was always kept wound up tight, and he was certainly a match for any five animals on the farm. But none of them, he felt sure, would dare to attack him, for they could only fail, and his punishment would be swift and sure. Besides, they had been pretty quiet lately. Evidently they had given up hope of ever defeating him. Even old Whibley hadn't made a raid in two days.

So at seven thirty that evening, leaving John Quincy

and X in charge of things, Grover, accompanied only by Lemuel and Eliphalet, pulled the levers that made Bertram walk, and steered him for Centerboro.

It was a pleasant walk, in the cool of the evening, with an important banker at the end of it, and Grover's mind was filled with dreams of empire when he mounted the steps of Mr. Weezer's porch and rang the bell. A little old lady in a sunbonnet opened the door and dropped him a curtsy, and ordering the two herons to stand guard outside, Bertram strode in.

And at the sight Mrs. Blench, leaning panting on the windowsill, with her nose to the pane and her eyes goggling almost out of her head, fumbled with shaking fingers at her fountain pen.

Mr. Weezer's front parlor was a good deal like Mr. Weezer: that is, it had not changed its appearance much in fifty years. There were a lot of black-walnut chairs with slippery horsehair seats, and a large center table covered with a red table-cover, and a whatnot containing a collection of minerals Mr. Weezer's grandfather had collected. There were some crayon portraits of some very forbidding-looking people, and there was a bunch of gilded cattails in a blue jar. There was also a stuffed owl over the mantelpiece. And in one of the chairs was a brand-new fire-extinguisher—

one of the brass cylinder kind with a handle at one end, which works like a pump that you pump up tires with.

"Good evening, sir, good evening," said Mr. Weezer, coming forward and holding out his right hand.

"Good evening," said Grover. And his right arm started to move and then dropped, and he held out his left hand. "You will excuse my left hand," he said, "but the right one doesn't work well."

Freddy, hiding behind the door, stifled a groan. He felt sure that Grover, always very correct, would rather take the chance of having his right arm throw Bertram's machinery out of kilter than offer his left hand. However, he had several tricks yet to try.

"Lovely weather we're having," said Mr. Weezer, as they sat down. "I don't know when I've known it to be finer."

So they chatted a few minutes about the weather, and then there was a tap on the door and Mr. Weezer's housekeeper brought in a tray.

"I thought you might like some refreshment after your walk," said Mr. Weezer. "Perhaps a cup of tea? And a little cake?" He handed Bertram a cup of tea, which the clockwork boy took in his left hand, and then passed him the cake.

Now, this was a very clever trick of Freddy's, I think. For in the first place, Grover, priding himself on his good manners, would be anxious to show that he knew how to manage a cup of tea and a piece of cake without setting anything down on the table. And that is one trick that you can't possibly do with one hand. And in the second place, one of Bertram's best tricks was eating things. Of course he was all clockwork inside, but his mouth opened and shut, and when you pushed a piece of cake in, his mouth shut behind it, and there it was on a little wooden tray, all ready for the engineer to eat if he wanted it. As for the tea, if Bertram drank tea, it just splashed down on the clockwork and did no harm, because the wheels were of brass and couldn't rust.

Well, Bertram took the cup and saucer in his left hand, and then his right hand came up a little way as if to select a piece of cake. There was a pause, and a click inside Bertram, and all the hidden animals held their breath, and Mr. Weezer's glasses nearly fell off, and if Grover had been looking at the stuffed owl over the mantel he would have known something was wrong. For the owl blinked rapidly three times.

But then Bertram's right arm sank down, and he said: "Thank you, no. No cake."

"What, no cake?" said Mr. Weezer.

"No cake," said Bertram firmly. "And, thank you, no tea. I've just had my supper, and I couldn't eat a thing. I hope you don't mind?"

"No, no," said Mr. Weezer hastily. "Certainly not." And he looked pretty unhappy. For he had tried twice, and failed, to make Bertram move his right arm. And the third and last trick which Freddy had thought up was one which he had protested against for a long time before agreeing to have it tried.

Mr. Weezer talked on awhile about the weather, but he was so nervous that he took a large bite out of his saucer instead of his piece of cake and had to go out and get another one. And when he returned he got terribly mixed up. "Yes, yes," he said, "the weather, now. Such a lot of it as we've had! Day after day, nothing but weather, weather, weather. I don't know what people are thinking of, to be sure."

"Weather never affects me," said Bertram, and then suddenly he sat up very straight. "What's that?"

Mr. Weezer's front parlor had two windows on Winker Street, and two doors: one into the hall and one into the back parlor. And suddenly at each of the windows appeared a red glow that grew brighter every second, and heavy smoke, shot through with bright flashes of flame, poured in at the doors.

Now, if there was one thing Grover was afraid of, it was fire. For Bertram was made almost entirely of wood. And he was a year old now, and good and dry from sitting month after month up in the loft.

Bertram jumped up and went to the hall door, but the flames flared up brighter, and he dashed for the other door, only to be driven back into the room.

"Can't get out here!" called Mr. Weezer from the window. "Flames are licking the windowsills. Get the fire-extinguisher!" And suddenly he toppled and fell in a heap, as if overcome by the smoke.

Now, it was only the animals burning red fire at the windows, and burning newspapers in washtubs outside the doors. But Grover didn't know that. He saw himself trapped. He thought he could probably get through either the doors or the windows, but he saw there were flames there, and if a flame got one good lick at Bertram, there would be no way of putting him out. And without Bertram he could not rule the F.A.R.

There is only one way to work a fire-extinguisher, and that is with two hands: one to hold it, and one to pump. Bertram picked the extinguisher up and turned it on the door. But he hadn't pumped it more than twice when there was a loud click inside him, a whir and a rattle, and then his right arm seemed to go crazy. It whirled around three times, smashing Mr. Weezer's chandelier—which wasn't a very pretty one, however —and then grabbed his left leg and tried to pull it off. Then it did several other odd things, while inside Grover tugged frantically at the levers, and finally it did the thing it had done once before—it reached around behind and opened the little door and pulled the operator's tail-feathers.

Immediately the wasps swooped from behind the crayon pictures on the walls, and although the door shut again, there were ten of them inside with Grover. It was more than flesh and blood could stand—even the flesh and blood of imperial Grover. He wrenched open the door with a claw and flew out into the room, and the wasps followed him—not stinging, but merely buzzing and circling until they had driven him cowering into a corner. And old Whibley, who had been posing as a stuffed owl over the mantel, dropped down and held him with one claw until the animals came in out of the hall.

Bertram was lying on his face, thumping the floor heavily with his right arm. Ronald climbed into the little control room and managed to quiet him down. The room was full of smoke, but there was no fire to

be seen, and Mr. Weezer was standing by the whatnot, panting with excitement.

"Congratulations!" he said to Freddy. "As one
bank president to another, I've never seen a smarter
piece of work."

XIX

At ten o'clock that night Bertram came clumping up the stairs to the loft. The place was in an uproar. Eliphalet and Lemuel had returned a little earlier with a story of having been driven from their posts on Mr. Weezer's doorstep by a party of eagles, and of having watched from a distance the destruction of Mr. Weezer's house—and of course of Mr. Weezer and Bertram—by fire. The party of eagles was Vera, who, because she could see in the dark, had been able to make short work of the herons. And the destruction by fire was a slight exaggeration, due to the herons' anxiety to tell a good story.

A silence fell when Bertram came up the stairs, and John Quincy said: "Father! We were just about to send out a rescue party."

"There is no need, my son," said Bertram, with his voice turned up so high that it was impossible to tell whether it was Grover's or not. "A dastardly attempt was made on my life, but it has been foiled, and the conspirators will be punished. Eliphalet, and you, Lemuel, you deserted me in my hour of need. Go! Never let me see those beaks again!"

The herons looked at each other.

"That's gratitude for you!" said Eliphalet.

"Well, it's all right with me," said Lemuel. "I never did think much of this job. Boy, will I be glad to get back to the swamp!"

"Me too," said Eliphalet. "The heck with this military rank and martial glory. A couple of nice shiners for supper, and then a good snooze on one leg. Come on, Lem." And the two walked to the window and spread their wings and disappeared in the darkness.

"Father," said John Quincy, "let me take your place tonight in Bertram, and you perch on the rafters and get a good night's sleep."

"No!" shouted Bertram. "Go to bed, all of you. Staff meeting and general audience at dawn, as usual."

And he sat down in the chair.

The birds, after whispering together for a few minutes, settled down and tucked their heads under their wings. But Simon, who had been looking a little puzzled, lifted his chin at Ezra, and followed by their entire family, the rats went down to the feed-bin, where they had taken up residence.

Now, the feed-bin had a cover, and the whole bin as well as the cover was lined with tin. When Grover's decree had given the rats the freedom of the feed-bin, they hadn't bothered to build for themselves in the barn any of the winding tunnels with many exits which are so useful in time of trouble and which make it so hard to drive rats from a barn they have once settled in. They had been so sure that Bertram would always keep the upper hand that they had merely got him to raise the cover of the bin. And here they were all now gathered.

"Children," said Simon, "there is something strange going on. Something queer. I don't like it."

"In other words, Father," said Ezra with a laugh, "you smell a rat."

"It is no joking matter, son," said Simon. "When Bertram came in just now, there was a tail-feather

246

sticking out of the little door in his back. And it was not a woodpecker's tail-feather."

"Father!" said Ezra. "You don't mean—?"

"I mean—" Simon began. And then he stopped. "What's that?" he asked sharply, for a faint giggle had come out of the darkness beyond the feed-bin.

Simon made a jump for the edge of the bin, but he was too late. With a bang the cover came down, shutting them in as tightly and as hopelessly as if they had been locked in the vault of the Centerboro National Bank. And Jinx's voice mocked them. "Sleep well, my little darlings," he said soothingly. "Jinx is watching over you. Jinx is right here. He will stay on the top of the bin all night. Good night, my little dears."

At dawn, as the birds took their heads out from under their wings and shook themselves, they saw Bertram still sitting in the chair. They ranged themselves in a row on the bench, and after a while Bertram said: "John Quincy, beat assembly."

So John Quincy went over to the door and drummed assembly on it with his beak.

Grover had established a strict discipline in his army. Within three minutes they were lined up in the barnyard and ready to march, and many of the other animals, too, had roused at the sound of the drumming and come out to see what was going on. Then Bertram went to the door.

"Soldiers," he shouted, "you have served me well and faithfully. But I have come to see that the sacrifices which war entails are too great. You have worked hard—too hard. No empire is worth such labor. Therefore I dismiss you. Go to your homes. Let us give up this dream of empire and cultivate the arts of peace."

There was a lot of excited cheering from the army, for most of them hadn't found it such fun to march half-way across the county and back every day just in order to say that another state had been added to the F.A.R. But John Quincy and X were astonished.

"Why, Father," said John Quincy, "you just passed a law yesterday about military service for rabbits and some other animals. What will we do with them when they report for duty?"

"What was the law?" asked Bertram. "Repeat it to me."

"Why, I don't remember exactly," said John Quincy. "Do you, Xie? Only it was rabbits and—and chickens, I guess. They have to serve three months, or was it five?"

• • • With a bang the cover came down • • •

"It must be a pretty poor law," said Bertram, "if you can't remember it the day after it was passed. I declare that law repealed. I declare all laws which I have made since I came into office repealed, and all orders void."

Hank was standing with the rest down in the yard. He had a feather stuck in his mane. It looked like a woodpecker's tail-feather.

"Do you mean I can go back and live downstairs in the barn, like I always used to do?" he asked.

"You can," said Bertram. "And the mice can come back, and the chickens can go back into the chicken-house. The rats—"

"Down with the rats!" shouted Charles, and a number of the animals drew away from him, looking scared, for the rats stood high in the new government's favor.

"The rats are guilty of conspiracy," said Bertram. "They have been imprisoned."

At this there was a great whispering among the members of Grover's staff, and one of the hawks said: "Mr. President, with all due respect, the rats are our most able military advisers. We should be lost without them."

"Yes, Father," said John Quincy, "listen to Cecil.

You can't mean to punish them. What did they do?"

"Silence!" said Bertram, turning on the woodpeckers. "My orders for you are to proceed at once to Washington, and to wait there until I come."

"But, Grandfather—" said Xie.

"At once!" said Bertram, and as they still hesitated, he picked them from his shoulders with his left hand and tossed them out of the window into the air, where they circled once or twice and then flew up into the elm, to talk excitedly together.

"Now, my friends," said Bertram, "I will ask you one question. Are you pleased with me, or do you still want to go on with the conquest of more and more territory for the F.A.R.?"

"Good for you, Grover!" the animals shouted. "No more war. Let's go back to the way we used to live."

"Very well," said Bertram. "And now I will tell you that it is not Grover who is speaking to you; it is Ronald. Last night, under the leadership of Freddy, and with the help of Mr. Henry Weezer and a company of wasps, we captured Grover. We have banished him, and he will not return. Since he no longer controls Bertram, he no longer holds the power. And I am at last at liberty to invite our real president, the one whom we elected, and who will run this farm in

Mr. Bean's absence, to enter into office. Ladies and gentlemen, animals, birds, insects, and hoptoads, I give you Mrs. Wiggins!"

And through the ranks of happy and shouting animals Mrs. Wiggins came slowly forward. There were tears in her eyes when she faced them—good big honest tears, such as only a generous-hearted cow like Mrs. Wiggins can shed.

"Well, dear me," she said, "I must say you animals have gone through a lot to make me your president. So I guess the only thing I can do is to be as good a one as I can. And I expect the thing I'd like you to do best is to just go on doing the things you want to do, as you always have. As for you, John Quincy and X—" She looked up into the elm. "Oh, well, they've gone. Just as well, I guess. So now, animals, I thank you. I guess that's all I've got to say."

An hour or so later, Freddy went down to the bank, to see how things were getting on. He was outside, busily painting the words: "For Animals Only" under the bank's name on the sign, when he heard a faint tapping on the roof of the bank, and looking up, saw John Quincy and X sitting there watching him.

"Look, Freddy," said John Quincy, "we don't want to go back to Washington. Father's going to be pretty hard to live with after this defeat. He's always terribly grouchy when his pride is hurt, and this has hurt it bad. Couldn't you keep us on as clerks? We'd look after things. You wouldn't have to get here at all if you didn't want to—"

Freddy looked up at them thoughtfully. It certainly would be nice. To be president, and have no responsibility at all. And then he thought: "Responsibility! That's what Mr. Bean thinks I have. It would be letting him down to try to get out of responsibility. And anyway, could I really trust those two?"

He picked up his paintbrush and drew two thick lines through the names of John Quincy and X.